Ouija

Book Two of the PIU Series

EK Dobbins

Apellez Dreams Publishing

Illinois, USA

EK Dobbins/Apellez Dreams Publishing
5343 Belleville Crossing St
PMB 75
Belleville, Illinois 62226
www.apellezdreamspublishing.com

Publisher's Note: This is a work of fiction. Names, characters, places, and incidents are a product of the author's imagination. Locales and public names are sometimes used for atmospheric purposes. Any resemblance to actual people, living or dead, or to businesses, companies, events, institutions, or locales is completely coincidental.

Book Layout © 2017 BookDesignTemplates.com

OUIJA/ EK Dobbins. – 3rd ed.
ISBN 979-8-9877350-0-8

Contents

CHAPTER ONE

The Grand Leyman Hotel and Casino

A massive building with countless protrusions and impossible additions juts out in random angles, reigning over an otherwise flat landscape. The tallest portions reach five hundred stories into the night sky. Glass and unearthly metal alloys make up the glistening façade. It is also used as a backdrop for advertisements for sponsors of the many events, past and present, held inside of the galleries of the massive building. As large as a metropolis, the Grand Leyman Hotel and Casino boasts up to two million rooms. Almost all of them are full for the three-week Mystical Paranormal Convention hosted within the halls of the futuristic style fortress.

Robotic bodyguards escort high class patrons from the drop off point all the way down the winding sidewalk to the entrance of the hotel. The trek is two miles and filling the void on either side of the wide pathway is a crowd of angry onlookers yelling and screaming at those that dare take the journey.

A flimsy barricade of aluminum fencing and non-mechanical police officers' line either side of the pathway to keep the protesters at bay. Loud music and evangelistic speech blends into the cocktail of raging voices. Drones of all shapes and sizes fly or walk around the horde in search of anyone willing to talk with them about the events both inside and outside of the hotel.

A slight figure meanders confidently down the winding sidewalk as she makes her way towards the towering doors of the hotel. She decides to take her time despite arriving later than she'd planned. The start of the transportation strike in her home district did not help with her timing, yet she did arrive before she has to teach her class.

Her bracelets jingle as she carelessly weaves her way through the mob of reporters and fellow patrons of the convention. A cluster of media robots attempt to stop her for an interview along the way. She either ignores them or politely declines and increases her step to distance herself from the media pod.

A gentle breeze catches in her naturally curly hair, exposing the colorful band that holds it back from her delicate face. She is traveling in comfort, wearing her favorite jeans, sneakers and bright red leather jacket. Her lilac eyes dart around the crowd as she continues her way, silently observing the derogatory signs brandished every seven feet. She is mostly intrigued by the strange uniformity of the faces within the crowd, filled with equal amounts of rage and terror.

A group of crazy-eyed men jump emerge from the crowd and push their way past the barriers. Some of the men wrestle with the police officers as at least six of them race towards the lone woman. She swears at the unprovoked attack as she takes a step back and calls upon her gifts. The attacking men stop moving and stand in place as if in a trance. Numerous fellow demonstrators scream and point upward prompting the traveler to focus upon the area of terror.

A second woman leisurely levitates to the ground and lands, softly, upon her feet She is wearing the uniform of the new Paranormal Investigation Unit. Her blood red hair is now tied in a bun on the back of her head with a couple of stray strands fanning in the wind. The woman's facial features reflect full annoyance as she studies the now-frozen men.

The traveler holds her ground as the PIU officer turns and faces her. The officer's blood orange eyes gleam in the twilight as a slight smirk tickle onto the right corner of her lips revealing a very sharp vampric tooth.

"Bun venit, to the Mystical Paranormal Convention," the officer said to the traveler. "I am Lt. Deloris Matox, PIU."

"Vă mulțumesc pentru primire," the traveler responds, much to the officer's surprise and delight. "I am Chancellor Monroe."

"Ah, the speaker for the Tarot Manifesto class," Deloris smiles. "I hope to be able to attend, it sounds fascinating."

"It would be an honor to have you," Chancellor Monroe said with a nod. "What are you going to do with those six?"

"No need to worry about them," Deloris said as two regular officers' step forward. "These two will escort you to the hotel. I will see you tomorrow."

"Till tomorrow then," the chancellor acknowledges.

The traveler turns to see that most of the protestors have fled the area once the PIU officer landed. The two large policemen flank the professor as she starts to walk to the hotel once more. Several of the officers on the sideline salute them as they continue their way. The professor glances at the two and notices that they are high ranking officers and appear to be in a trance.

The giant glass doors of the hotel swoosh open as the trio approaches. The police officers stop and hold their heads, shaking them as they seem to now come to their senses. The noise and the sight of the bewildered men disappear once the doors shut behind the traveler. She smiles, hoping that the room she is occupying has the same level of soundproofing as the lobby. The demonstrators outside show no signs of leaving anytime soon.

The long line to the front desk did not surprise her, this event is very popular for practitioners and non-mystics alike. Her eyes train to the wall behind the desk with a slight whistle of admiration.

The Mystical Paranormal Convention takes up all seven of the enormous conference rooms offered by the hotel. Each looks to be the size of an old-fashioned department store. The overflow of the convention, to include an authors' room and meditation areas, take up the large suites located on the first twenty floors.

The gambling machines, usually in the middle of the hotel, are replaced by an army of vendors. The machines now occupy a small area on every lobby of the upper floors, conveniently near the elevators. The only things that remain in place on the first floor are the various restaurants and main kitchen of the hotel.

A historical marker shows a point of interest that occupies a much smaller hall past the vendor area.

Different colors on the map designate classrooms that are scattered throughout the entire hotel, even some on the topmost floor. The traveler crosses her arms as her features twist into annoyance at the map. She hopes that her room is close to the teaching space else she will have to test the teleportation spell she just learned a few days ago. A group of giggling arrivals push past her and get into line to purchase tickets and check into their rooms.

The professor frowns at the line then looks at her travel receipt and smiles. She lifts her head proudly as she approaches the clerk that has no one in line, the VIP check-in counter. The robotic courtesy clerk lights up with a joyful beep when it senses the arrival of the traveler. The default green screen with lines change to a pleasant, yet very artificial-looking, female face grinning at the guest.

"Good afternoon, ma'am, and welcome to the Grand Leyman Hotel and Casino. Host of the Mystical Paranormal Convention," The robotic clerk chimes politely. "Please state your name so that I may assist you."

"Jesse Monroe," the woman said in an even tone.

The screen flips to several dots as the computer processes the information. Jesse contemplates the technology that the hotel uses, she knows there are better robo-clerks on the market. She suspects that the owner of the hotel is thrifty. A full minute passes then the screen once again lights up, this time with the picture of a brown skinned woman dressed in a professional suit. Her hair is similar to the way she is wearing it today, tied back by a green band to match her suit. Her lilac eyes sparkle with a lifetime of experience, despite her youthful appearance. Jesse smiles at her picture.

"Please confirm your identity by placing your hand upon the picture," The robo-clerk instructs.

"Yes, that's me," Jesse acknowledges and places her palm on the screen.

The screen flashes between red, yellow and green as it confirms the identity of the guest. A strange noise emits from the machine and the screen goes blank. Jesse hisses and hastily pulls her hand away when she feels a small current course through her body. She shakes her hand as she frowns at the robotic clerk. Her scowl becomes a look of curiosity when a ghostly image fades onto the screen. She is unable to tell if the image is male, female, or even if it is artificial. The screen immediately flips back to the helpful robo-clerk, stopping any further study of the ghost within it. The image smiles as the screen buzzes, becoming fuzzy. It then solidifies back up once again.

"Thank you, Ms. Monroe. Your room is free of charge complements of this year's sponsors," the robo-clerk cheerfully announces. Two items pop out of slots on the counter. "Please proceed to the Old Town section, suite 50065."

"Let's see. Oh! A map, how quaint," Jesse said sarcastically as she examines the items in her hand. "Although this will be helpful, I am requesting a guide. This is, after all, my first time visiting your hotel."

The robotic clerk grins as the screen flashes out, her face disappearing. An old-fashioned silver desk bell fades into view. A ding emits from the mechanical being causing Jesse to roll her eyes. An answering sound surprises her and she turns in time to see a short silver robot whiz efficiently across the polished marble floor.

The robot is shaped similarly to an exclamation point, with a large dark ball on the bottom as an omnidirectional wheel. A red bellboy cap is sitting on the top and flashes red as it comes to a stop in front of Jesse. The size of the entire bot did not reach past Jesse's shoulders. A professional logo graces the broadest part of the bot, proudly displaying 'Sponsored by No-Ghost Inc'. Jesse contemplates calling the sponsor, especially after her encounter with the ghost within the robo-clerk.

"Hello, Ms. Monroe. I am Bellbot 75, the greatest guide within the Grand Leyman Hotel and Casino." The robot boasts in a boyish voice. "I will be escorting you to your room today! Would you like me to gather your luggage?"

"My luggage should already be here," Jesse said as she places a hand upon her hip. "I am expecting a package sometime this evening or early morning. Once it is here, take it directly to the classroom."

"Yes ma'am," the bellbot exclaims excitedly as it whirls around happily. "Shall we proceed to your room?"

"Lead on," Jesse acknowledges.

The bellbot circles around Jesse twice and heads straight for the hall. She follows the excited robot at an unhurried pace. A smile touches her lips, the mechanical being reminds her of several students back home. She could imagine their enthusiasm if they had accompanied her to this convention. Stepping over the threshold from the foyer into the main hall of the convention causes Jesse to hesitate.

The entire place is teeming with folks from all manner of backgrounds around the known universe. Many of the practitioners had decided to wear garb associated with their particular mystical art. Others had settled on more elaborate costumes depicting their favorite character from movies or books. Jesse takes a deep breath then starts to mix into the crowd of patrons.

She is able to get through the hall and enter a spacious amphitheater that connects the various sections of the hotel itself. It is the size of twenty city blocks. A multitude of passageways stretch out from the central point into various unknown locations within the hotel. A holographic billboard floats above the crowd, pointing towards various conference rooms, ballrooms, suites, restaurants, and recreational areas available to all guests of the hotel. Vendors crowd every possible space and leave very hardly any room for people to flow by.

Jesse looks around for her guide, finding that she has lost him within the vast network of people. She merges with the flow and takes the opportunity to look around at the various offerings of the convention. She pauses by a vendor when she sees a hardback book boasting to contain 10,000 ancient spells and curses. Jesse engages in conversation with the young saleslady when her bellbot kindly bumps into her to get her attention. The professor grumbles under her breath and apologizes to the young lady as she resumes her journey.

The crowd and vendor booths eventually thin out as Jesse continues to follow the bellbot. She hesitates when the mechanical being appears to be going down a darkened hallway. Her senses warn her not to proceed after Bellbot 75. A loud ding is heard from the darkness as the bellbot turns around and comes to re-trieve Jesse.

"Ms. Monroe are you well?" The bellbot inquires.

"I'm fine," Jesse assures. "I'm just not so sure about going down this hallway."

"The lights that are usually on recently blew out," The bellbot explains. "A maintenance bot has been assigned to replace the blown bulbs. I have escalated that ticket to be done as soon as possible."

"And my room is through this hall?" Jesse inquires.

"There are elevators on the other side of the hall that we will use to go up a few flights to your room," the bellbot said. "It is a small portion of this hallway that is dark. The rest of it is bright and cheery."

"And ghosts?" Jesse asks.

"Don't worry! My No-Ghosts shield will keep us from being bothered by any wayward spirits should they be present," the bellbot said with confidence.

The robot cheerfully circles around Jesse twice then heads down the hall once again. Jesse clenches her jaw as she considers her options then reluctantly follows the mechanical being. The quiet hum of the robot's motor is swallowed by the unyielding darkness. The overhead lights buzz as they try to illuminate the space did not produce enough light to see a couple of feet in any direction. Jesse glances about and pauses when she sees people walking with a slight jerking motion all around her.

Many of them are dressed for the medical profession. Mixed in are a couple of people wearing strange tie-on gowns. The majority of the people had endured some sort of trauma. Jesse sidesteps to avoid of the strange beings as they seem to not see her. She wisely quickens her pace to get to the end of the hallway. A bright light beckons her to hurry as soft voices start to echo about the hall. She exits into the light then takes a quick look around, breathing a sigh of relief when she sees no strange spirits wondering the void. She also notices that her guide is missing.

"Now where did it go?" Jesse scans the area and notices a second tunnel next to the one she exited. "Perhaps there."

A chill goes down her spine prompting her to turn to face a would-be threat. Her jaw goes slack at the sight that presents itself. It is a small grey stone church and grave yard. The stones have darkened with the onslaught of age and weather.

Beautiful stained-glass windows reflect the damage done through pollution, sunlight, and unknown environmental factors. Tiles are missing from the roof. The tall steeple no longer hosts the grand bell that beacon those who worshiped within the small hall. Gravestones sticking up from the concrete marks where the faithful now rest on the right side of the building.

A large, heavy, rope marks off the area to keep visitors from entering or destroying the historic and fragile monument. Jesse closes her mouth and shakes her head. Never in a million years did she expect to see the small grey structure inside of the Leyman Hotel.

She walks to the front of the building in order to stare into the open door. Her surprise multiplies when she sees that the interior appears to be in perfect condition. Soft light imitates sunshine from above, illuminating the structure. Streams of light beam through the windows and doorway as if beckoning patrons to enter.

"What in all.... a church?" Jesse exclaims her shock, loudly. She walks around the structure just to be sure. "They built this hotel around a church?"

"It appears that way," a small, childlike, voice agrees. "A complete church with some minor damage that can be repaired. I suppose I could add it to the collection."

"Bellbot 75?" Jesse looks around.

An orange blur flashes in her peripheral vision. Jesse locks onto it then swiftly face the perceived threat. She sees nothing but a black striped tabby cat sitting on a fencepost. He has a yellow bowtie on and a dress suit made for cats.

The feline grins at her and tilts his head as he focuses his yellow-green eyes on the startled woman. Small, white feathered wings flutter in time to the playful wave of his furry long tail. His hind legs are as white as his wings, giving the illusion that he wore fluffy socks. Jesse studies the small, intelligent, face and relaxes with a slight grin as she gazes into his human-like eyes.

"Ah, so you are a seraph cat," Jesse acknowledges the creature. The cat lets out a happy sound.

"I am!" the cat says and holds out his paw. "I am Nako Sothpaw. Pleased to meet you, Miss..."

"Monroe," she answers and lightly takes the paw in her hand. "Jesse Monroe. It is a great pleasure to meet you, Sir Nako."

"Oh! I've heard many good things about you," Nako chirrups, "Your thesis on telekinesis was great! Many of my comrades within the known universe were impressed."

"Thank you," Jesse says, a little blown away by the accolades.

"Why are you in this part of the building? The convention did not span into this section as far as I'm aware of," Nako tilts his head to one side with a look of concern.

"I was following Bellbot 75 to my room but must have lost it in the tunnel," Jesse thumbs behind her at the dark passageway. "I don't particularly want to go back in there to look for my guide."

"Yes, dark places give me the creeps too," Nako shudders at the thought. "I've been to this hotel often enough. Perhaps I can point you in a less ominous direction to your destination. What is your room number?"

"I have it right here," Jesse pulls out her ticket. "Old Town, room number 50065."

"Well, it's not on the top floor, that's the good news," Nako grins. "Even better is that your room is right next to mine. I'll show you the way."

The seraph cat crouches and wiggles his backside as he flexes his wings. He jumps into the air and uses the feathered appendages to glide a about two feet out before landing perfectly on all four paws. His fluffy tail lifts high as he trots towards the lighted hall left of the church.

Jesse lets a soft chuckle to escape her as she watches the enthusiasm of the regal feline. The hair on the back of her neck stands on end. All humor disappears as she faces the intruder. She is taken aback when she sees a man previously undetected staring at her from the doorway of the church.

Large, feathered wings spread wide behind his well-chiseled form. Jesse makes eye contact with the man and stumbles back a step. She shakes her head to clear it then looks back up to study the man. He is now gone.

Jesse gawks at the empty spot, unable to comprehend what she had just seen. He was not a spirit or wayward ghost but seemed to be something associated with the essence of the church. Jesse jumps when she feels a little bump on her leg.

"Are you alright, Jesse?" Nako asks when the young woman focuses on him.

"I...think so," Jesse admits and gently rub her arm. "I might need a coffee or strong tea before I go to my meeting tonight."

"I have one too, about some sort of training software they want to premiere here," Nako said as he walks towards the hall again.

"The same," Jesse nods and follows the cat. "They call it, Ouija. I gave my opinion, but they seem to want to discuss it among those they sent samples to."

"Ah, so we are in the same meeting. I've read the documentation on it. There are too many loopholes and unexplained experiments that went into the making of this program," Nako scowls. "I too gave them my answer, however, if they want me to give it in person, I am very willing to do so. Not to mention that this meeting is an extreme waste of time."

Jesse smiles as the seraph cat continues to fuss, speaking his mind about the meeting and its inhabitants. As he talks, her own mind wanders back to the encounters she has had so far in the hotel. The strange face upon the robotic clerk screen pales in comparison to the spirits that wander the darkened hall.

The last encounter at the church is the one that sticks out the most to her. She has never encountered an angel before. However, he did resemble what she's read about in various divinity texts during her studies. Jesse considers to rationalize the encounters once she has the proper rest or after the meeting this evening.

Nako turns the corner and keeps a slow and steady pace so that his guest can keep up with him. Jesse takes the time to look about, noting that they have once again returned to the main hall of the event. Many of the patrons laugh and have a good time as they show off the latest incantation they just learned. An older mage cuffs his apprentice in the back of the head to prevent him from summoning a demon as Nako and Jesse walk past them.

A trio of ghosts dressed in roaring twenties attire glide through the crowd, unfazed by the No-Ghost shield tower. The mechanism did not make a peep. Jesse studies the slender tower and finds the on/off switch.

It is currently on, and the power light indicates that it is working yet something is malfunctioning within it. She looks around to see at least thirteen No-Ghost towers standing in various locations of the convention hall. Jesse makes a sound of contempt as she continues her way, easily catching up with Nako.

The sounds of busting dishes in the kitchen echo in the hall they take as serving bots rush by carrying all kinds of meals and drinks for the patrons of the hotel. Jesse nibbly avoids the swinging doors as a large bot with multiple trays bursts forth from the kitchen and heads to the convention floor.

Nako pauses in front of the gift shop and sits down, tilting his head to one side. A large statue of the Egyptian goddess, Bastet, sits right at the front of the store staring out at all visitors. Jesse stands with Nako and admires the statue from her position.

"It looks very detailed, who was the artist?" Jesse inquires.

"I don't know," Nako answers. "The statue is a replica of the one in my museum, but much bigger. I need to stop here for a minute to get a snack before we go upstairs."

"No problem, I'll wait here," Jesse says.

Nako goes into the store as Jesse looks about, noting that some of the patrons are heading down the hall to their rooms right now. She glances at her watch to see that nightfall is starting to set in. The sound of sniffling catches her attention. She looks up to see a little girl huddled next to the wall a short distance from the gift shop. The child's back is to the traffic and people walk past her as if she is not there. Jesse frowns at the attitude of the attendees, then sighs and goes to check on the child.

"Hey, are you alright?" Jesse asks as she approaches the girl.

"I'm so sad," the girl sniffs.

"Why?" Jesse frowns then notices that the girl is transparent. "Oh.... Crap...."

"I'm sad...because...." The girl sniffs again as Jesse takes a couple of steps back. "You are going to die!!"

The girl whips around and sneers. Her face is half burnt, much of it missing. The child's eyes are filled with madness as she launches herself towards her victim. Jesse quickly draws a symbol in the air and activates it. A portal opens just in time to swallow the ghost and closes within a few seconds.

Jesse folds her arms, her features reflecting her full displeasure at the experience. The sound of applause breaks Jesse from her brooding thoughts as she faces her impromptu audience. Nako pushes to the front of the group and sits down.

"What happened, Jesse?" Nako frowns. "Did I miss a performance?"

"No, I was attacked by a child ghost," Jesse said as the audience disperses. "Do you know the owners of No-Ghost Inc.? I have some very unkind words for them."

"It is a group of men, none of them are familiar with the world of the paranormal but they have an advisor," Nako said. "The advisor himself is questionable. We can talk to a partner of the organization at the meeting. I'm not sure how well he will listen, but it is worth a try. We will go to the elevators and then to our rooms. It's not too much further."

"Thank you, Nako," Jesse nods to the cat. "I'll try to rein in my frustrations before I sit down for the meeting."

The service elevator dings as it arrives on the fifth floor of the hotel complex. The doors open to allow three robots and two living beings to exit into the hall. Jesse looks back and forth to see that the passage stretches for literally miles in both directions. The halls, just like the one where she lost Bellbot 75, are dimly lit, creating a very creepy atmosphere.

Nako stretches, patting his front paws on the floor, then continues to walk towards his room. Jesse looks about once more then cautiously trails after the regal feline. A short walk down the hall and she pause when she feels her foot squish onto a wet rug.

Jesse swears and looks down, allowing more unladylike words to escape her. The rug is now filled with blood from wall to wall. Jesse looks up and manages to keep her third set of unkind words to herself when she sees a man hanging from a ceiling that no longer exists. His neck is pierced by a meat hook, eyes wide open in surprise. Jesse shakes her head and moves away from the apparition then searches for Nako. The seraph cat has continued down the hall, oblivious to the hanging man. Jesse turns back to see that the apparition is now gone, and the floor is back to the original color.

"Nako," Jesse catches up with her guide, "do you know what was here before the hotel was built?"

"The small church is still here so that's one thing," Nako answers and pauses in front of a door. "I did read about a meat factory that was once on the grounds. It was closed when an inspector discovered that the owners were selling human meat to other humans."

"Well, that explains the hanged man, but not the trapped medical staff," Jesse contemplates.

"Hanged man?" Nako scans his surroundings. "Where? I did not see one."

"He was about ten steps from the elevators," Jesse explains. "I've lost count of the number of encounters I've had since my arrival."

"Maybe one or more practitioner downstairs is stirring up ghosts and spirits with their demonstrations." Nako said, his tail waving, contently.

"They should know better," Jesse holds her head.

"You would hope," Nako agrees. He points his tail to the door. "We've arrived."

The door is made from synthetic wood and designed to look like it came out of an old castle. Jesse approaches her room as she pulls out her keycard. The numbers on the card and door sync up with a green glow to indicate a match. She places the card into the slot just under the numbers then backs up a step and waits.

The screen that displays the room numbers goes blank with several dots crossing from left to right. After a short time, it lights up again with a small keyboard and instructions to enter the last five digits of an identification number. Jesse obliges and the screen blanks out once more. An audible click comes from the lock and the door opens.

Jesse takes a deep breath and enters the room cautiously. She deliberately exhales in a calming way when she notes that it is freshly cleaned with a hint of lemon upon the air. The bedsheets are pressed and folded down to invite the guest to sleep.

A large bouquet of flowers now occupies the bed with a note-card dressed in a pink envelope. A curious look crosses her face as Jesse studies the flowers. Her eyes train to the back of the bed and a smile graces her lips when she sees that her luggage has arrived in one piece.

Jesse once again focuses on the flowers as she ponders who would provide them in her room. Perhaps it is a tradition of the hotel to greet guests with a bouquet? She's heard and partici-pated in some strange rituals yet this one is a little disturbing even to her.

"Nako, is it a tradition for the hotel staff to leave flowers for the guests?" Jesse inquires.

"Hmm?" Nako squeezes pass the young lady to look at the dis-play. "What? No, I did not get flowers or catnip when I first arrived. I think you have a not-so-secret admirer."

A stern look crosses Jesse's features as she walks confidently into the room. She holds up her hand as she heads to the couch. The envelope levitates from the bed and flies to her outstretched fingers. She feels a strong energy that she did not care for from the letter as she sits down. Nako hops up to sit next to the young woman as she opens the envelope and reads the note inside.

Jesse's features go from surprise to contempt as she reads the steamy words and suggestions contained within the letter. It is signed by Kalup Leyman complete with his room number and time he expects her arrival. Nako sneaks a peek over her arm to read the note as Jesse stares at the wall in contemplation. A small silver flame leaps from Jesse's palm to the letter, consuming it hungrily. Jesse stands and goes to the window to look out as Nako taps his tail and furrows his brow in deep thought.

"Nako, will Mr. Leyman be at the meeting?" Jesse asks, her voice holding mild agitation.

"This is his hotel, so I believe so," Nako guesses. "He's also co-sponsor of both this event and the program we are to review."

"He wants an answer for his letter, I will give it to him when I see him," Jesse promises.

"I looked over your arm at the letter and did not like what I saw," Nako admits. "He mentioned your school, what is going on there?"

"We..." Jesses takes a deep breath in and out as she goes to sit back down on the couch. "A megachurch was recently built by a radical evangelistic group called 'The Faithful'. Because of their harassment, my attendance has been low."

"They are the same group that is demonstrating outside," Nako frowns.

"There was also a recent visit from Senator Harry that, I'm afraid, did not go as he planned," Jesse crosses her legs. "He wanted me to hire questionable friends of his wife as well as some other dealings that he did not mention when I refused."

"Knowing Peter, it was something that would gain him more political prowess," Nako rubs his chin with his front left paw. "How long has your college been in business?"

"It was founded by my ancestors about 5000 years ago," Jesse answers proudly.

"I'll have to make a few calls, but I think your college qualifies for our historical locations program," Nako said. "The political environment has changed quite a bit since Senator Harry took the reins. Cheer up! We will help you get through this little storm in your life."

"I appreciate it, Nako," Jesse said as she bends down and places a hand upon the feline's back, gently.

"You are very welcome! We can discuss your college in more detail after the meeting. By then I will have my answer," Nako purrs and arches his back against the hand in a clear indication of enjoyment. "I am going to meet my friend, Dr. Louis, then head to the meeting. Did you want us to escort you there?"

"No, I think I will rest here for a bit then meander there in about an hour," Jesse assures him and stands up. "I will find my way. Thank you for the kind offer."

"I will see you there," Nako chirrups and heads to the exit.

Jesse opens the door for her guest to let him out. Nako hesitates in true feline fashion as he debates if he wanted to leave. He sits in the middle of the door and looks around, meowing softly. Jesse smiles as she waits for him to make up his mind. A minute later, Nako takes the steps to leave the room and Jesse closes the door as she chuckles.

A holographic television, holotube, pops on as she walks past the desk. She puts it on mute as fast as she can when she sees the story. The news is on and currently shows an overly eager young journalist, in a cheap skirt suit, interviewing some of the demonstrators outside the hotel. Jesse puts the remote down an makes a few comments about the scene. She is not in the mood to hear any of the incoherent ramblings of the 'faithful'.

The exhaustion of her day is starting to catch up to Jesse as she yawns and stretches in the middle of her room. She scratches an itch in the middle of her back and eyes the couch. It seems to beckon her to fall into the folds of the cushions. Jesse flops down and sprawls out, one leg on the couch the other dangling to the floor, as she stares up at the ceiling. Her mind wanders over the encounters she has faced today.

The maddened child seems to stick out the most with the angel encounter falling into a close second. Jesse relaxes a little as she thinks about the two very different spirits. Her eyelids grow heavy, and she allows them to close as she surrender to sleep. The soft whirl of a camera as it focuses on the young woman goes unheard as Jesse snuggles down to get more comfortable within the cushions.

The sounds of a ringing phone as well as the vibrations from it wake Jesse from her slumber with a start. She blinks and shakes her head to complete her waking and takes out her phone to look at it. She sits straight up as she reads the message from one of her associates. She is distracted by a noise coming from a short distance to her left. Jesse glances over as a voice whisper from inside the bathroom. A soft glowing light accompanies the voice as well as small spirts of childish laughter. Jesse stands up with a frown on her features as she walks over to the bathroom door.

"Oh, not this room too," Jesse grumbles. "I swear, if this space is haunted, I will call in all the girls to exorcise this place."

The bathroom light comes on as soon as she gets close enough to enter. The illumination is pale and ghostly as shadows retreat to the corners of the room. Jesse peeks into the bathroom and scans it. A pristine toilet, sink and inviting white soaking tub with elegant light grey shower curtain greet her. Jesse uses caution as she step into the bathroom and relaxes. She tunes into all of her senses as she studies the entire area.

Her attention goes to the pristine ceiling and fan when she detects a small whirl from it. She notices a red light but does not pay much attention to it, as long as there are no hanging apparitions. Jesse is careful to tears her gaze from the ceiling to the shower wall and tilts her head in curiosity.

Words or an image appears to be on the wall, making it look dirty. Jesse stares deeply into the tile and waves her hand over it in an attempt to force the image to reveal itself. The blemish disappears as if something is holding it back from the curious woman. Jesse arches an eyebrow then glares at the wall; flames come to life within the depths of her eyes.

The wall responds by pulsating purple and white repeatedly and at rapid pace. Jesse releases her influence, yet the wall continues to pulse wildly. A woman screams insanely as she jumps out the wall towards Jesse. Hollow eyes burn with blue fire as long spindly fingers reach for the living woman's neck. Jesse drops an unkind word and holds up her left hand to erect her arcane shield.

The ghost slams into it and scrapes it with her nails, red drool exits the wraith's mouth before she disappears. Jesse hesitates a few seconds then lowers her ward, folding her arms as she recalls the quick interaction. This is the second time in this hotel that a ghost has become violent towards her. She also notes that the specter wore a nurse outfit like the ones that wonder the passageway near the convention halls. She concentrates on the shower wall once more and sees nothing out of the ordinary.

"Oh, yeah, being unhappy is an understatement," Jesse grumbles out loud.

The lights in the bathroom pop off when Jesse exits it in a stride that reflects her displeasure. She muses at the 'No-Ghost Inc.' logo located throughout the convention and resolves, with conviction, to send in a complaint. Jesse takes a look around the main area and nods as she makes a decision. She will leave this hotel as soon as she is done with the meeting and go to the nearby Ghelby Bed and Breakfast, if they still have room. Jesse glances at the clock on the wall, noting that she still has some time before the meeting.

"Well, no more napping in this hotel," Jesse said. "I'll need to request my luggage to be transferred after I take care of a few minor things tonight."

Jesse goes over to a mirror and tidies up her hair then straightens out her jacket before she leaves the room. She does not notice the reflection in the mirror watch her leave then transform into the nurse specter that attacked her earlier. Jesse closes the door and hums a playful tune as she heads down the hall to the main elevators. After a long hike, she finds them located in a lobby full of slot machines.

Jesse pushes the button for the elevator to go down, humming as she waits. Her senses scream danger, and she turns around to face it. A young man that is dressed up as a comic book warlock curse and goes around Jesse to get onto the elevator as the door opens. He holds the door open politely enough though his features hint at the opposite. Jesse hesitates then decides to take the stairs down. The young man scowls as he releases the elevator and gradually fades into the light. The elevator doors close as it stays in place.

CHAPTER TWO

The Meeting

The buzz of the conference does not slow down but seems to increase in activity as the night settles in. Jesse wanders through the hall for a few hours to look at the various offerings of each vendor. She notices that several of them are selling the same merchandise at vastly different prices. Yet, they are spaced so far away from each other that there is no real competition amongst them. Jesse settles in at a book vendor and discusses various journals upon the table. A couple hurries past the book booth pushing all their merchandise as they head for the front lobby. Jesse watches them then notices that several of the vendors are closing shop and packing up for a hasty departure. She excuses herself from her new friend and goes over to a vendor that is almost done with disassembling their booth.

"Excuse me," Jesse said. The elderly woman that is addressed pauses in her hasty packing.

"I'm sorry, but we are closed," the woman answers automatically. "We will not be back, but you can visit us in the next convention if you survive this one."

"Survive?" Jesse frowns.

"This place is cursed. It is evil," the elderly woman stands from her box and looks Jesse in the eyes. "A dark force in the guise of a mortal has control over those who were consumed by the flames of madness. Beware and leave this hell hole as soon as you can."

"I did see specters while traveling through the hotel," Jesse recalls. "The encounters have me agreeing with you."

"You've not even touched the tip of what is crawling in the very mortar of this building," the elderly woman assures her and hands Jesse a card. "Whatever you are here for, cancel it and leave. It is not worth your life."

The elderly woman's male helper picks up her box and places it on a cart. The two then hurry to the exit of the building, nearly colliding with several patrons in their haste. Jesse watches them for a short time then looks at the card presented to her. She recognizes the Chariot from a deck of Tarot cards. Jesse turns it over to see the name of the elderly woman: Sophie Malkin, Head Sister of the Clairvoyants of Old Salem Temple.

Jesse crosses her arms; this has reaffirmed that she will be departing the Grand Leyman and perhaps head home to work out issues at her school. The entire area quiets a as a chime goes off and a female voice announces that it is 8:00 p.m. Jesse looks at her watch and frowns before heading to the elevator.

"I will at least say my goodbyes to Nako," Jesse muses.

The elevator dings as it reaches the twelfth floor. A large group of party goers rush to get on, scarcely allowing the passenger that currently occupies it off. Jesse expresses her relief at surviving the onslaught as she takes in her new surroundings. As shown on the map, the convention continues all the way up to this floor and beyond. Like the other lobbies, slot machines are relocated here to accommodate the event. Gamblers of all ages squander their money on a chance for riches.

Jesse glances at a map to verify her location and faces a large security bot next to an ornate door. The mechanical being takes its time to lift off the ground as she approaches. Red LEDs light up where the eyes are located, and a warning ding sounds from the speaker that represents the mouth. Jesse shows her invitation and waits for the security bot to scan the item. The LEDs turn from red to yellow then green as it acknowledges the participant.

"Welcome to the meeting, Ms. Monroe. Mr. Leyman has gone to the front desk in order to escort Senator Harry to this meeting, so it has not started yet," The robot said in a cold, mechanical, voice. The door opens. "Please enter and take your seat. Refreshments will arrive shortly."

"Thank you," Jesse acknowledges. "Can you radio for a bellbot to retrieve my luggage and mail it back to my home? I will be departing after I talk to my companion."

"I will relay the message to Bellbot 75," The security bot replies.

Jesse nods her response and enters the room. The door closes behind her as she examines the other participates in the meeting. A stately blonde woman glances at the latecomer with her light green eyes. She is wearing the uniform of the Paranormal Investigation Unit although the jacket is currently dangled across the back of the chair. It is apparent that she finds Jesse very disinteresting and once again focuses on her prior distraction.

Jesse follows her line of sight to a teenage boy balancing a book on his nose. He has a big grin plastered across his face that causes Jesse to smile as well. The scrawny boy adds a precarious backwards lean to his chair and waves his arms to maintain balance. His shoulder length black hair shifts back and forth as he works to keep the book on end.

Jesse nods in appreciation of the young man's skills until she catches movement out of the corner of her eye. Nako waves again at his new friend and pats the table next to him. Jesse acknowledges the invite and goes to sit next to the dapper feline. He is now wearing a tuxedo along with his bowtie.

"You look very nice, Nako," Jesse complements.

"Thank you! I was getting worried about you. Did you get lost?" Nako asks and tilts his head in curiosity.

"No, I..." Jesse starts, then shudders as if cold water is dumped down her spine.

Jesse moves to face another woman that she previously had not detected. This woman is unhealthily thin, her skin folds in several places as if it is unattached to her bones. Despite her apparent health issues, she has a strong authoritative air about her. Her nut-brown hair is pulled up into a perfect bun, not even a strand is out of place. Eyes the color of orange flames dance in glee as she meets Jesse's gaze. Jesse tilts her head then turns

 EK Dobbins

away to clear her mind. A frown comes to her features as she tries to determine if the gaze is an attack or if her overstimulated senses are messing with her.

The door to the room opens again, this time for a young man with a large computer tucked under his right arm. He appears agitated, the acne rash that covers his cheeks and neck flush extra dark red as if to reflect his mood. He hurriedly places the computer on the desk and runs his fingers through his short black hair as he opens it up and turns it on. He takes off his large, thick-framed glasses to clean the lens with a cloth he pulls from his pocket. He then uses the same cloth to wipe his brow, blows his nose, then places the cloth back in his pocket.

He returns his glasses to the bridge of his nose and glances around the room nervously. A look of relief crosses his features as he realizes that the special guest has yet to arrive. The thin woman leans over and speaks quietly to the young man, patting his hand as if to reassure him.

The unmistakable sound of belligerent masculine laughter echoes in the hall as the door opens. The blonde in the room glances at the entrance then stares as two men enter the room. The first to enter the room is tall, well dressed, and devilishly handsome. His black suit is a perfect fit to highlight his lean, yet strong, frame. His light brown hair is pulled back into a sophisticated ponytail and frames his handsome face in the form of a goatee. His dark green eyes focus on Jesse and a roguish grin deliberately spreads across his features. Jesse meets his gaze, showing very little emotion.

"That's Kalup Leyman," Nako whispers. Jesse nods to acknowledge the cat.

The second man, Senator Peter Harry, that entered the room had a bright smile upon his face at first. It soon turns to a scowl of discontent as he looks around at the occupants of the meeting. His dark grey suit is hard pressed to contains his muscular arms and chest. The front buttons are straining to keep together yet he does wear it well.

The lights bounce from the polished dark skin of his bald head. His black eyes reflect his displeasure of not seeing certain people in the room. The teen takes the book off his nose and places all four of the chair's legs back on the floor. Nako yawns, already disinterested in the two men. The strangely thin woman and young programmer stand up, prompting the rest of the room to do the same. Nako climbs onto the table in front of his seat and sits down, defiantly.

Jesse meets Peter's gaze when it falls upon her, then follows it as he turns towards the blonde. The woman twists her lips as if to force them together and not spill any secrets. Peter opens his suit coat and pops it as he marches over to a large throne-like chair at the head of the table. He sits down and leans back to get more comfortable.

Jesse follows the lead of the other guests and once again takes her seat. The second man places his hands behind his back as he stands next to his special guest. Jesse crosses her legs and arms as she sits back. So much for leaving early. She resolves to leave as soon as the meeting is over with.

"Ladies and gentlemen, welcome to the Grand Leyman Hotel and Casino but most importantly, the 300th anniversary of the Mystical Paranormal Convention. I am Kalup Leyman," the standing man says as he glances around the room. "The gentleman with me is our noble guest, Senator Peter Harry. Since this meeting is being recorded for future reference, can you all please state your names and organization that you represent?”

“Christine Longstraw, on official leave of absence from the PIU and representing the National Coalition of Rouge Witches,” the blonde introduces herself first. Then she turns to the thin woman in the room. “My constituencies are impressed by the software you are presenting but had several concerns that I hope you will address.”

“I,” the teenager says, as he places his phone on the table in record mode, “am Doctor Louis Lygtbut. I was asked by our lady, Queen Arayna of the Aligons, to represent our interests in this rudimentary software. Truth told, she does not like it at all, the subject is complicated, yet the approach taken with this program is way too simplistic in her opinion.”

“The Queen and I share similar views,” Nako acknowledges and touches his collar. A small green light pop on. “I am Sir Nako Sothpaw, Head Curator of the Museum of Past Modern History as well as knight and representative of the Galactic University of Mystical Artists.”

“You represent GUMA?” Christine asks, surprised.

“I do indeed,” Nako said, proudly. “And like it or not, Christine, in the absence of your fellow PIU officers, you are the face of that unit.”

“Diana is here, she should bring her ass to the meeting instead of whatever she’s doing,” Christine snorts in discontent.

“I’m sure that an incident within the halls has taken precedence over the meeting, considering that the hotel is filled with violent ghosts," Jesse says as she places her phone on the table, also in record mode. "I am Jesse Monroe, Owner, and Head Chancellor of the Monroe College of Metamorphism. My understanding is that this was a meeting of the minds over a program that did not appear fully thought out. The minds have spoken, we do not care for your product."

"I visited your school not too long ago and it appears that you still have not learned your lesson in being humble, Ms. Monroe," Peter said, rudely. "Your opinion means nothing to me."

"Well said, Senator Harry," the strangely thin woman applauds with a grin. "I am Irava Javou, and this is my IT guru, Ronan Neard."

" 'ello," Ronan grunts but keeps his focus on the computer screen.

"Now that this tedious introduction is done, I want to see the demonstration," Peter informs the group. "I need to go to my next meeting that I am already late for."

"You are demoing it?" Jesse arches an eyebrow.

"The majority of opinions in this room are rubbish and unfounded," Irava said. "There is absolutely nothing to fear from this program. I back this product a hundred percent both physically as well as financially. Ronan, can you please introduce and demonstrate our little project?"

Ronan rolls his eyes as he gets up to stand in front of the door to face everyone at the table. They young man mutters under his breath as he fumbles in his pocket to find a remote and uses it to bring up a holographic slide show. The title of the slide, Ouija, is the same as the name of the software. Ronan describes that the program's main objective is to train users to bring forth and control the spirits from the astral realm. This also include so called higher beings such as a variety of deities.

Jesse places a hand upon her temple and closes her eyes in an attempt to stave off the headache she is now experiencing. Every single word from the young man seems to add to her misery. Nako coolly plays with Jesse's bracelets to curb his boredom. She glances at the feline and smiles at his expression; he has already mentally left the room.

Louis stares intensely at Ronan, analyzing the young man as the slide presentation continues. Christine leans back and closes her eyes, ignoring the presentation. Kalup focuses strongly upon Jesse and smiles when she, bit by bit, faces him and meets his gaze, unflinching. Peter exhales loudly as he glances at his wrist-watch.

"You have ten more minutes of my time," Peter announces, interrupting Ronan. "Do you have the software, or will you bore me to death with a slide show?"

"The slide presentation is to give you the background information for the program, Senator Harry. Do not be in a rush," Irava said.

"Ten minutes," Peter reiterates with an undertone of irritation.

Jesse watches as Irava tightens her jaw as her resolve hardens. A strange energy radiates from the thin woman while she stares at the senator. Peter glances at his watch once more and glares back at the woman. Irava turns her attention to Ronan and nods once. The young man gleefully sits down at his computer and cracks his knuckles.

The slide show disappears as Ronan brings up his holographic keyboard. Louis leans over to watch the young man and scowls from some of the words he sees. The lights in the room start to dim, catching members of the audience by surprise. Ronan finishes his typing and slaps the enter key. The humming of large computers coming online fills the void of silence. Jesse jumps as the wall behind her starts to lift, revealing several arcane supercomputers. The colorful LEDs blink and flicker as they finish booting up and accessing the hotel's internet. The beeps and hums of the various fans sound almost like the droning of human voices in chant.

A shudder goes down Jesse's spine and her hair stands on end from the sounds of the machines. Christine hisses as a cold feeling envelops her. Miniature holograms of several styles of Ouija boards float into view, rising from the table. Louis sits back and rubs his chin as the programmer stands up. Ronan pokes the hologram of the original Ouija board causing all the other variations to disappear. Peter grumbles impatiently as the spectacle continues. Movement in the corner catches Jesse's attention and alerts her. She faces it in time to see a ghostly light float over towards the computer then disappear into the light fixture of the room.

"This isn't good, we've got to stop this," Jesse says to Nako.

"Irava, I think we have seen enough," Nako says. "This program has to stop, now."

The warning is not heard over the humming of the machines. The selected board increases to the size of the table and lowers into place. Both Jesse and Nako jump when they hear a solid thump from the action as the board connects to the tabletop.

Louis touches the part closest to him and mutters words his mother would not be proud of under his breath; the board even feels real. The letters light up on the board, as if they are made of fire as a wooden planchette shimmers into view. Christine shakes her head in disbelief at the entire process so far.

"First, I would like to thank you, Sir Sothpaw, for having such an elaborate and well-preserved collection of Ouija boards in your museum system." Irava says as she holds up a glass to toast the curator. "We went through great lengths to replicate each and every board. I am especially proud of this one."

"These are replicas of the boards housed in the Museum of Witchcraft. This has made me highly concerned," Nako says as his fur bristles. "Those boards are infamous for a variety of reasons. You obviously did not get my permission to replicate them, I would have recommended against it."

"I've visited the museum several times in my career and am familiar with the boards located within," Jesse volunteers. "I do not recognize this one as part of the collection."

"I've been there too, it's not in the collection," Christine says. "I don't like the looks of this."

"This is one that has been in my family for many generations," Irava boasts.

"It looks cursed," Louis points out.

"It might have been at one time, but not anymore," Irava shrugs. "Ease your concerns, we have everything under control."

"I am very confident that Irava and Ronan are in complete control of this program," Kalup says with assurance. "I've seen them run it many times with no consequences."

"That might explain all the paranormal activity in your hotel," Jesse retorts.

"I would like to invite either Ms. Monroe or Ms. Longstraw to take the software for a little spin," Irava says with a smile.

"Have you lost your mind? Hell no, I don't want to participate in your demonstration," Christine crosses her arms. "I don't like the looks of it, or the smell of it. I think you need to stop this bull-shit now."

"I will have to agree with Christine and likewise decline to participate," Jesse said.

"I will add my voice to those that are calling for this demonstration to come to an end," Louis speaks up. "Or at least pause it until we find Officer Hunter since Officer Longstraw has refused to represent the PIU."

"We have just a few more minutes of Senator Harry's precious time, there is no room to search this hotel for a wayward detective," Irava concludes, sarcastically. "Besides, Christine summed it up in the beginning. Officer Diana Hunter should have been here."

"I'd have preferred Officer Matox," Nako said, honestly.

"I'd prefer neither," Peter said and perks up. "How do I start this thing?"

"It is primed and ready to go. Just direct a question to it," Irava explains.

"The staff has informed me that the hotel has ghosts," Kalup says and nods to Jesse. "Ms. Monroe has recently verified this. Perhaps you can summon one of those."

"You do not need this software to experience any of the ghosts here," Jesse says. "And I will vehemently advise not to summon any of the ones I experienced in this hotel. All of them have exhibited violent tendencies towards the living."

"You are in no rank or position to advise me, Ms. Monroe. Keep to your peers or you will see your school closed due to your lack of tact," Peter said to the woman.

"You've already put a choke hold on the funding for my college, Mr. Harry," Jesse reminds him, anger filling her words. "You still owe me a written explanation as to why."

"I will be the voice of reason then," Nako said as he places a calming paw on Jesse's hand. "I am familiar with the other Ouija boards and could have provided guidance to safely use them. This one needs to be studied before it is used. Peter, do not use this thing without knowing the consequences first."

"I can provide the guidance," Irava says. "Remember, it is my family's heirloom. I will guarantee that it is very safe to use. Almost like a boardgame of sorts, except you summon spirits. If you like, think of it as your personal genie."

"I see," Peter sits back, confidently. "Ouija board, if there is a ghost in the room, who is it?"

The sound of the machines fills the silence of the room for several seconds. The tempo of the hum fades down to a tolerable level. Nako's fur stands on end as the planchette on the Ouija board starts to move, scraping against the wood grain ominously. Christine swears and Jesse echoes her words as the planchette inches, jerkily, over to the letter 'C'. it hesitates for a moment then makes its way over to the 'H' near the center of the board.

It slides to the letter 'A' as Jesse stares at it. She looks around and sees the ball of light that had occupied the corner earlier, hovering just above the Ouija board and appearing to control the planchette. Louis sits back and studies the entire board as the handpiece finishes spelling the name of the ghost, lining up with 'R-L-I-E' in sequence.

Jesse stands up as lights flicker around the room, noticing that now more than one ghost seems to occupy the space. The hum of the machines increases substantially, forcing Christine and Ronan to hold their ears. A variety of unkind language flies from several members of the meeting as those still seated, except Irava, rise to their feet as the light coalesces above the center of the Ouija board.

Ribbons of ugly radiation swirl into a tight orb as a final flash temporarily blinds all in the room. Jesse rapidly clears her vision then must readjust her eyes to a persistently pulsating red glow that now fills the area. The dull clicking of metal against wood captures the attention of those occupying the room. Jesse drops a word, perhaps a prayer, as she stares at the entity. Nako lets out a fierce feline sound of surprise or fear from the sight.

The long belts that once tied around the specter to hold him tight are loose and dangling from the sleeves of a threadbare straitjacket. The rags of his tattered pants flutter in a non-existent breeze. Holes in his jacket show ribs as well as charred flesh. Overall, his exposed skin is dark gray and burnt, red eyes stare dully at Jesse. The young woman meets the specter's gaze as her mind travels back to the conversation she had prior to this meeting.

"Ronan, dismiss it," Jesse says as calmly as she can and without taking her eyes off the entity.

"Dismiss…" Christine rubs her eyes and adjusts them to the new lighting. She curses in quite an unladylike manor when she sees the ghost. "Have you lost your damn mind?"

"According to that jacket, he did a long time ago," Louis points out the obvious.

"You have your ghost, Peter, now give it a command," Irava offers, her voice overly calm.

"So, this is what a ghost looks like," Peter leans forward, hands touching the table, as he studies it. He is unaware that he is touching the holographic Ouija board.

"In my professional opinion, Mr. Harry, do not ask or command this spirit to do anything," Louis offers. "According to his ancient, tattered clothing, he was unstable in life. I doubt that has changed in death."

"I see it in his eyes," Jesse warns. The ghost grins at her.

"I am curious," Peter said. The ghost faces him, unhurried.

"Don't be," Christine echoes the warnings of the other voices in the room. "I've seen enough of these to know that what Louis said is true."

"Charlie," Peter addresses the spirit, ignoring the group, "What were you in life, and how did you die?"

The ghost, Charlie, continues to float aimlessly above the table as he studies Peter. An evil smile spreads across his dried lips as the unnerving sound of a soft mechanical click barely reach the ears of the living. The ghost throws back his head in manistic laughter as a rush of electricity fills the entire room.

Jesse grits her teeth to prevent any unclean language from escaping as all the computers go haywire. She then unleashes her words as she is spun around and tossed backwards towards a solid wall. Jesse manages to flip in midair to get her feet under her and land on the floor, sliding back just an inch.

Christine and Ronan both duck under the table to avoid the ghost. Nako yowls in surprise as a force throws him into the air. Louis jumps across the room, catches the feline, and rolls away from the danger. He stops a few short inches to avoid colliding into Jesse. The teenager positions himself and Nako behind the chancellor.

Charlie uses his belts to grab Peter and Kalup, wrapping the leather appendages around their throats. Blue and red energy dances down the belts and into the two victims. Kalup manages a yelp of pain as Peter gasps for air. Irava sits calmly at the table and sips on a glass of water.

"Quick! Get rid of it!" Christine demands as she shakes Ronan by the arm.

"OK, O-KAY! I'll try," Ronan stammers.

The programmer reaches up and grabs his laptop off the top of the table as Charlie continues to cackle. Ronan places it down and frantically types in commands on the screen. He cusses when one set of commands does not work and immediately tries another set. Those commands came back as an error code, yet the program continues to run. He hits the power button.

The machine hesitates a couple of minutes then sends another error stating that the it does not recognize the commands. On the verge of panic, Ronan snatches the battery out, killing the machine. The energy in the room does not falter and Charlie continues to be present.

"Oh, don't tell me that it's not working!" Christine screams.

"How do we dismiss the ghost magically?" Ronan inquires in a panic.

"Why are you asking me?" Christine does not hide her annoyance and shock.

Jesse does not hear the conversation as she concentrates her energy into her core. She crosses her arms and points her fingers skyward as a light sheen of purple energy caresses her form. Jesse lets out a mighty yell as she sends the energy from her form towards the ghost, breaking his concentration. The wild energy surges around the room decreases significantly as Peter and Kalup drop to the floor.

The senator coughs and catches his breath as he rubs his neck. Charlie sneers as he turns towards Jesse then shrieks in anger, sending his belts in her direction. They hit an arcane shield, much to the ghost's surprise. Jesse points to the ghost and utters three ancient words. Silver whips leap from the table and wrap around Charlie. The ghost makes brief eye contact with Irava before he is dragged into the Ouija board. Charlie groans as he disappears and the board shatters.

The pieces vanish before they hit the ground. Jesse lowers her arm as Ronan and Christine slide from under the table. The supercomputers whine as they shut down and the false wall gradually lowers back down. The lights in the room return to normal as Jesse exhales, calming her agitation. Louis places Nako back on the ground with care.

"I am leaving this building as soon as that door opens," Jesse grumbles.

"I think I will follow you out," Nako agrees. "I have to make a couple of phone calls now."

"I checked all nearby hotels, they are all booked because of this event," Louis informs them. "My workplace, however, has plenty of crash space and it's nearby."

"What in the hell just happened?" Peter demands as he gets to his feet, dusting off his jacket. "Irava, explain yourself."

"I want to know the same," Kalup scowls. "This did not happen when you handed me the trial, Irava."

"Of course, Kalup, you used the software to summon a seductress and you enjoyed it," Irava reminds him. "Senator Harry used the software for what the original Ouija board was built for, communicating with random spirits."

"Maybe the program was tampered with," Louis observes, then looks to Ronan. "Did you take proper precautions and place it on a secure network or was it on a public domain?"

"What are you insinuating?" Ronan snaps as he reassembles his computer. "I'm a professional! I know what I'm doing with security. Public, private, it does not matter because it is impossible to tamper with my program."

"If it is not hacked, then it obviously has bugs," Christine remarks. "That piece of software junk is unsafe as hell. I nor my constituencies will ever endorse that thing."

"We will take your feedback and incorporate them in the second release," Irava dismisses the worry.

"Do you understand the real-life consequences had I not banished Charlie from this plain, Irava?" Jesse inquires, annoyed. "This software should never be released; I recommend destroying it so that some foolish moron does not find it and try to use it."

"The authority to release lies with Senator Harry, not you, Ms. Monroe," Irava snorts in distaste and turns to the official. "Senator?"

"Before I can endorse this, I have to consult my peer, Senator Ludwig Worvog, and then I will let you know, in time," Peter said and fastened his suit coat. "Your time period is up. I have another meeting to go to that I am already late for."

"I would be honored if I could escort you to the front, Senator," Irava offers as she stands.

"No, I need to speak to Kalup on my way out," Peter said. "Come along, Mr. Leyman."

The door opens as Peter approaches it and walks into the hall. Kalup hurries after the senator, absorbed in a discussion with him about the other people in the room. Christine fusses as she leaves the room, and the door remains open.

Jesse calms herself down then turns to face Irava, noting that the woman is now studying her. Nako sits down and tilts his head as he watches the body language. Ronan let out a rash of foul language as he tries to program his computer and it errors out. Louis chuckles from some of the Aligon words the young man uses as swears.

"Sir Sothpaw, Dr. Lygtbut, do not let this snafu frighten you," Irava offers. "Other than this, I feel the software will be good for the future of all in the Known Universe."

"I highly doubt that it was a mere snafu," Jesse says. "After all of the spirits that I met in this hotel, that one is the most lethal."

"So, it's haunted, big deal," Irava shrugs it off. "Many places are haunted, perhaps this was built over an ancient burial ground."

"Jesse, remember we are at the Mystical Paranormal Convention," Nako reminds her. "Perhaps the demonstration had some interference from what is going on at the convention below."

"I'm not so sure that's true," Louis whispers and is silenced by Nako.

"Does this mean you endorse us, Sir Sothpaw?" Irava asks with a smile. Her skin appears to stretch as she does.

"You go to a curated museum and duplicate cursed Ouija boards in order to make your software 'sellable' to more nefarious clientele," Nako reminds her. "Then you, against the request of the majority of the room, demonstrate it on an unknown board, that may be cursed itself. No, Irava, I nor the Knights of GUMA will ever support or endorse this piece of litterbox waste."

Thunder roars in the room as an insulted Irava lashes out with a strong lightning spell towards Nako. Ronan swears and ducks into a corner to avoid any stray hexes. Jesse takes a step forward and blocks the bolt with hardly any effort. She holds the spell firmly as she spins around and sends it right back at the caster. She sends another, similar, spell immediately in the wake of the first.

The dual incantations speed across the floor, slicing through the table and aim straight for Irava. She cancels the first, however, the second slams into her harshly, sending her to the floor. Louis swears in an alien language as he moves back from the fray. Nako hastily joins him as Irava is careful as she gets back to her feet. The thin woman's features contort with anger as flames dance in her eyes. Jesse rolls her shoulders and faces the agitated woman. Irava's features turn from anger to humor much to Jesse's surprise.

"So, you are not a weakling like I thought," Irava chuckles as the table returns upright and stitches back together. Several chairs roll into place. "I should have known better. Will you stay so we can discuss the software like civilized witches?"

"You have some audacity to even suggest any kind of discussion," Jesse answers. "My opinion will never change about this extremely dangerous software, ever."

"We have more important meetings to attend as well," Nako interrupts any more violence. "As Senator Harry has said, your time is up."

Nako holds his tail high as he saunters through the threshold with authority. Jesse trails the seraph cat as Louis takes up the rear. The door to the room closes as Ronan starts to have a conversation with his employer. Jesse frowns as she walks the short distance to the elevator with her companions.

Aside from her physical appearance, there is something very otherworldly about Irava. Jesse goes over the meeting in her head and wonders if the thin woman is from a newly discovered portions of the Known Universe. The ding of the elevator brings Jesse back to her surroundings and the conversation between Nako and Louis.

"About this relic you want me to look at," Louis holds the door of the elevator for both Jesse and Nako. "Is it creepy and looks like it belongs in a horror film or novel?"

"Oh, it's not that bad," Nako protests. "It is the perfect place to make my calls and complete some paperwork. Jesse, I need a little more information about your school before I sign it into the protection program."

"I will give you any information you need," Jesse assures him as the elevator doors close. "I hate to make our encounter short, gentlemen, but I think I will be leaving after our meeting."

"We are also leaving the convention," Louis agrees.

"I just want to finalize things before we go," Nako explains. "I also want to see if I can locate Officer Hunter. It is very unusual for her not to show up for important meetings."

"I hope she's okay," Jesse says.

CHAPTER THREE

The Encounter

The elevator dings as it arrives at the ground floor of the hotel. Nako leads the way off, easily walking between the legs of those in a hurry to get on the vessel. Jesse and Louis dodge and push their way off the elevator, quickly catching up to the feline. Jesse hesitates when she notices that Nako is heading straight for the once semi-dark hall that she had traversed before. The lighting is better, yet the hall is still in twilight. Louis continues after his friend without breaking his stride. Jesse takes a deep breath in and follows Louis into the dimness.

In a few short strides, Jesse catches up to Nako and Louis halfway down the hall. The seraph cat has stopped in his tracks and his back is arching up, hair standing on end. Several specters continue to march through the gloom, apparently unaware of the living among them. Louis gawk at the ghosts then turns his attention to the hospital uniform they are wearing. He has never seen them before. Jesse is careful to avoid the ghosts as she arrives next to her companions. The wandering apparitions disappear as soon as they hit a strange new bright blue glow. Jesse notices that the light is coming from a No-Ghost tower.

"That is odd," Jesse muses.

"Those uniforms are odd," Louis counters.

Nako makes a break for the end of the tunnel, nimbly dodging the ghosts he sees and going through those he does not. Louis leans over to investigate a patient as he floats by on a stretcher. The patient is muzzled and tied down with a straitjacket, his dead eyes hold rage and madness within. Jesse gently touches Louis's shoulder to prompt him to follow after Nako. The hair on Jesse's neck stands up as she senses danger. She whips around to see the nurse ghost that attacked her in her room sneer and disappear back into the shadows. Louis stares at the area in wonder.

"Let's get out of here before she gets back," Jesse warns and picks up the pace.

"All the times I have been to this hotel, I do not recall ever coming down this hall," Louis says.

"Might be a reason for that," Jesse offers.

The end of the tunnel looms in sight. Jesse increases her speed, reaching her destination. She exhales as she exits the tunnel, stunned that she held her breath while traveling the last part of the hall. Nako expresses his relief when he sees his friends have survived their encounter. Louis is about to make a smart comment when his attention turns to the relic that Nako has led them to. Jesse silently watches with a confident smile on her lips as the doctor walks around the structure and stares up at the steeple. Nako sits down, his tail swishing with humor.

"Are you kidding me? A church? The relic is a church?" Louis exclaims.

"You had the same reaction as Jesse," Nako laughs.

"I think anyone who sees this small ruin would have the same reaction," Jesse said. "Where did you want to have the meeting, Nako?"

"Where else? Inside the church," Nako answers and walks nimbly towards the structure.

The seraph feline slips under the security rope and strides the small path that leads into the open doors of the structure. Jesse follows in his footsteps, ducking under the rope and taking her time going to her destination. She looks left and right, noting the graves that are left around the structure.

Many with names worn so faint that it is hard to tell whose final resting place is now encased within the hotel. Shadows hover several feet from the structure, as if afraid of what lies inside. Louis jumps over the rope and playfully taps Jesse on the shoulder as he jogs past her into the building. Jesse chuckles a little at the child-like prank and is last inside of the church.

The interior of the church is clean and clear of any kind of debris. Wooden pews still line both sides of the hall, leaving the row in the middle wide enough for four men standing abreast to walk down, comfortably. A closer look at the woodwork reveals swords with angel wings carved into the sides and back of the pews. The altar stands proud upon a large stage at the end of the aisle. A much larger blade is carved on the front of the altar with the addition of a halo over the wings.

An ancient dialect surrounds the columns and crown molding of the entire church. The ebony wood floor hardly creaks under the weight of the visitors. Jesse takes in the details then centers her attention on a statue of a winged man kneeling between twin choir boxes toward the back of the structure. The statue has his arms crossed; his unblinking gaze bore into the souls of those entering his domain. Jesse moves her eyes up to the stained-glass window above the statue to see the angel's likeness battling a strange rat-tailed monster.

"I wonder if you are the one that greeted me before Nako led me away," Jesse says to the statue as she approaches him. "Well, safe to say you're not a ghost. Probably just a part of my overly active senses."

"I think he has been kneeling there for several centuries, yet time has done nothing to his pigment or the stonework," Nako walks left then right of the statue. "He is in immaculate condition."

"I agree, and very realistic," Jesse comments.

"I wonder if the statue...no way...impossible" Louis shakes his head as his trained senses detect something that is highly unlikely.

"I've blurred the lines on the possible and impossible a long time ago," Jesse says with a shrug, then turns with Nako towards the pews. "What information did you need from me, Nako?"

"Well first," Nako says as he jumps up on a bench and sits down. "I'm going to see if I can contact Deloris. Then we will work on the papers for inducting your college into the museum system."

"Alright," Jesse nods and sits down next to the seraph cat.

Louis sits with them but continues to stare at the angel statue. The fuzzy curator is sitting with his tail waving back and forth as he listens to the ringing of a phone. The picture of the person he's calling fills up the space in front of him. Jesse recognizes Deloris, having met her prior to entering the hotel. Nako tilts his head curiously as the answering system picks up instead of the officer. He is about to leave a message when it hangs up.

"That's odd, I thought I had good reception here," Nako frowns.

"Maybe we should call her after we leave the hotel," Jesse offers. "What information did you need from me for my school?"

"Ah yes, since you will not be teaching your class, can you demonstrate to me Tarot Pneuma?" Nako sits up and tilts his head as he talks.

"I'd be delighted to show you," Jesse smiles the worry melting as she pulls out a Tarot deck.

Jesse sifts through her cards until she finds the King of Pentagrams. She makes a triumphant sound as she pulls it and places the rest of the deck into her jacket pocket. Jesse holds up the card and recites a few words before tossing it out into the floor. A flash fills the room, blinding Nako. Louis notices the statue's eyes dilate ever so lightly then blink. The light dies down and is replaced by a devilishly handsome man with dark hair and eyes. He strokes his beard as he stares at Nako.

The seraph cat's jaw is slacken with shock; the man looks exactly like the picture on Jesse's card. The king stands from his throne and presents his 'coin'. It is gold with a pentagram in the middle, the edges sharp and glistening. The king tucks his coin under his right arm as he walks over towards Nako. He pats the curator on the head, further shocking the cat, then takes Jesse's hand. The king bends down and kisses the back of her appendage before he disappears. Jesse now holds the card once more between her index and middle finger of the hand he had kissed.

"Wow, he was real," Nako exclaims.

"Yes," Jesse agrees. "My understanding is that if he is summoned during combat, he uses his 'coin' as a chakram."

"Maybe he should have stayed," Louis said.

"Why?" Jesse arches an eyebrow.

"Because the statue is alive," Louis answers.

"No way," Nako chuckles, "He'd be centuries old if he were. Even older than the oldest living Aligon that I knew, Kem. He was about five hundred years old before he died."

"I think a current mutual friend of ours is much older than that," Louis hints. "Have you asked Deloris her real age?"

"I'm not that brave or crazy," Nako dismisses.

"What are you doing?" Jesse questions the doctor.

"Taking a closer look," Louis informs. He approaches the statue.

"That may be a bad idea," Jesse warns, noticing the wings are a little higher than when they arrived.

Nako hops onto the back of the pew in front of him and balances himself as he sits down. His tiny wings wave curiously as he tries to figure out what Louis is seeing. Jesse leans onto the same pew and focuses her eyes to meet those of the statue. The steely grey orbs pulsate as if lightning flashes within them. The energy in the room heightens expeditiously and Jesse stands up as Louis reaches to touch the statue's neck.

"Louis, don't!" Jesse shouts.

It is too late, as a great hand of the large, winged man shoots forward and grasps the doctor with unnerving speed. Louis cries out in surprise as Jesse and Nako scramble into the aisle. The statue flaps his wings once, sending a strong wind through the church and causing Jesse to stumble backwards onto her rear end. She gets back to her feet in a flash as Nako arches his back, fur, and feathers on end. The winged man lifts Louis off the ground, raising his sword to point between the doctor's eyes.

"Do not touch me, boy," the statue says, annoyance ripe in his deep, brooding, voice.

"Holy tea and whiskers!" Nako exclaims. "A Guardian!"

"I can see that," Jesse assures.

"He's not a friendly guardian," Louis announces, summarizing his current situation. He squeaks when the blade comes closer to his nose. The sword hums and crackles with otherworldly energies.

"My disposition, good or ill, will depend on your answer as to why you are here in this sacred space," The guardian informs him. He pauses and puts his sword aside, drawing Louis towards him, too close for comfort. "You are not human as I first believed."

"No, he is not," Nako says, moving forward towards the perceived threat. He smiles when the guardian shifts his focus from Louis. "You are also in the presence of a talking cat. We are here in this lovely temple to discuss what transpired outside of its walls. I am also musing adding it to the Galactic Registry of Historic Sites."

"I see, both you and this creature are not a natural part of this world," the Guardian said as he shakes Louis.

"As of nine hundred years ago, they are," Jesse informs him. She places a hand on her hip as the Guardian focuses on her. "Please put my friend down."

The Guardian stares at Jesse for a short time then drops Louis. The doctor lands on his feet and retreats, in a hurry, from the six-and-a-half-foot winged man. Jesse remains focused on the Guardian as her friends return to her side with Nako just a step behind her. Jesse places one hand behind her and causes a single tarot card to appear; the Knight of Swords. The Guardian flexes his wings and draws himself up as if to intimidate her.

Jesse remains still as the winged man scans her once again then turns his attention to the wall with a stained-glass portrait of a woman as if to compare the two. Jesse takes the opportunity to take one step back, prompting her companions to do the same. She knows that this Guardian is a very powerful being. If it is to come down to a fight between them, Jesse will have to find a way out of it and fast. A second card, The Magician, also appears in her hidden hand.

"By the name of the Mother," the Guardian turns his gaze from the glass as he rubs his closed eyes with his free hand. "What has this world come to since I've started my meditation?"

"Depending on when you started, many things, Lord Guardian," Jesse answers.

"One is that this church is now in the belly of a giant hotel," Nako said.

"Excuse me?" The guardian arches an eyebrow. "What...are you?"

"I am Nako, curator of the Museum of Past Modern History and the most handsome seraph cat you will ever meet," Nako introduces himself. "My home world was destroyed centuries ago and my ancestors harbor here on our new home of Earth."

"We Aligons were here a just a hair longer than the seraph cats," Louis said and takes another step back. "The history of how we got here is not peaceful nor do I wish to go into the narrative of it tonight. I am sorry I disturbed you."

"And what of you, Spellcaster? Are you also an immigrant to Earth?" the Guardian asks.

"My family and I are what you call natural citizens of Earth," Jesse answers. "And you, Lord Guardian?"

"I am as you said, a Guardian," the winged man smiles, humored. "You have a similar aura about you to the woman whom this sanctuary was built and dedicated to. This building marks her grave. I am her Guardian and have been so for over five thousand years."

"I am sure she is at peace," Nako said.

"What happened to her?" Louis asks.

"She...was claimed by the Flames of Madness. I had to..." the guardian trails off as his wings lower, indicating his continued sadness.

"Flames of Madness...?" Jesse frowns as she recalls a conversation earlier in the night.

"She called me Aegis; I was her shield." The Guardian says as he puts his sword away then turns his back.

"I think we should remove ourselves and find a different venue to discuss our meeting," Louis suggests. "I vote for Tanglewood."

"Good idea," Nako nods and turns towards the exit. He flips his tail back and forth as he trots towards it.

Jesse listens as her companions ultimately decide to go down a lighted hallway. She places the two tarot cards back into her pocket and turns to follow them. The energy in the room has damped with Aegis' sadness. Jesse is just four steps away from exiting when she senses a warmth coming from her right side. She turns and faces the window that the Guardian had mentioned. Jesse approaches it, as if being drawn to it, and studies the intricate details of the window.

It depicts a serene young woman with dark skin and a glowing smile. Her dark brown hair is tastefully braided, just long enough to brush against her shoulders. She is on her knees with her hands together in prayer, eyes lowered. Transparent wings wrap around her form with a white tunic keeping her modest. The scene around her is a peaceful countryside, large trees decorated in fruit and singing birds frame her with a small church just above the woman's head. The clear glass at the top of the window reflects the lighting of the chasm outside the building.

"She's pretty," Jesse remarks, catching the Guardian's attention once again. "I know she would be very unhappy if she was aware, you are bonded here."

"The bond I have here on Earth is that which I have done to myself," Aegis replies. He is now standing behind Jesse. "You remind me of her."

"Then you should know better than to sneak up behind me like that," Jesse said. She exhales as she represses the urge to punch the Guardian.

"Apologies," Aegis grins and moves back to give the woman room. "I did not hear your name, Spell Caster."

Jesse turns and glances over the Guardian as she walks past him. She stops by the pew that she had occupied with Nako and picks up her phone. The Guardian crosses his arms and smirks as the woman pockets her device and then once again focuses upon him. Jesse turns and walks until she is a step away from the door then faces the Guardian again.

"My name is Monroe," she says. "Jesse Monroe."

Jesse smiles and leaves the church as Aegis stares at her back. He shakes himself out of his stupor and goes over to the stained-glass window of the woman. He touches it as he studies the features closely. His eyes train above the woman's likeness and a frown comes to his features. The light of the day is no longer shining through the window. Aegis decides to leave the church and finds that he is now in a large, cavernous, hall. An explosion and jolly laughter from the passageway behind the church captures Aegis' attention. He decides to go investigate the sounds.

The noises of merriment increase as Jesse makes her way down the most lit hall in the entire hotel. She pauses by the elevators and turns to see she is not being followed. A ding comes from the elevator, capturing her attention. Jesse faces the doors as they open, and Christine Longstraw exits the carriage. She seems pleased at whatever activity she just had left; her skin flushed with her excitement. Christine ignores Jesse as she turns and walks towards the conference down the long hall. Jesse calls to her as she catches up to the woman.

"What the hell do you want?" Christine snaps.

"That's one hell of a greeting," Jesse responds. "I just wanted to know if you have encountered any paranormal activity before and after the Ouija demonstration."

"Why do you care?" Christine continues to be snappish.

"Because as an officer of the Paranormal Investigation Unit, I'd think you should at least report the encounters to your colleagues," Jesse says, feeling her blood pressure rising.

"Let me reiterate what I said in the meeting," Christine faces the woman. "I am on vacation. If you want to report something like that or someone did something stupid, you go find Diana. She's around somewhere."

"Maybe you can call her," Jesse quips, her eyes flashing with agitation.

"Are you challenging me?" Christine sneers as electricity courses through her being.

"Girl, you don't want to go there," Jesse retorts as her body starts to illuminate.

"Break it up! Break it up!" two security bots rush over with flashing lights and chanting. "Requesting assistance from Officer Hunter."

Christine snorts in distaste before she turns, flips her hair, and walks away. Jesse glares after the woman as she crosses her arms. She makes a sound of frustration, tosses her hands a little, and storms down a different path to get to the convention. The security bots quiet their alarm and start to wander around the hall once again.

Patrons' and vendors' laughter filter into the side halls of the hotel with ease. Jesse steps onto the main floor and notice that the haunted hall is across from the one she had just exited. She shakes her head at the labyrinth of halls and chasms that make up the Grand Leyman Hotel and Casino. She strolls into the vendor area as she continues to calm down from her encounter with Christine.

A ball of flame crosses in front of Jesse, causing her to stop in her tracks. She had been so involved with her own thoughts that she nearly collides with the performer. The firebreather apologizes to her for almost burning her eyebrows off. Jesse smiles and shows off a little flame magic of her own, causing it to dance a in the palm of her hand before she snuffs it out. She gives a slight wink to the performer and walks away. He laughs and complements her as she continues her exploration.

Jesse turns her mind to searching for her friends so they can leave together. She did not have to wonder long as a loud whistle catches her attention. She turns to the sound and smiles as Louis waves at her from a table at a fancy restaurant. Nako does a small happy dance as Jesse approaches the table, dodging a gaggle of unsupervised teenagers as she does. The restaurant has temporarily renamed itself to the Brass Goat during the three-week convention. The menu and prices, however, have remained the same. Jesse scratches Nako behind the ears as she sits down next to him. The seraph cat makes happy chirping noises as he leans into her attentions.

"I had forgotten about the reservations I had at this restaurant until they reminded me," Nako said. "I figured we should at least have a full tummy before we depart. Especially since you have a long trek home, Jesse."

"You are very thoughtful, Nako," Jesse responds to the cat.

"Nako also insisted that we do not order anything until you arrived. I was about to organize a search party to find you," Louis says in mock woe. His stomach growls to signify his hunger.

"Sorry, I had to find my way and had a run in with Christine," Jesse explains. "I'll make it a point not to talk to that woman in the future."

"I tried to call Deloris again and did not get an answer," Nako says and pauses when his collar jingles. "Now who's calling me?"

The curator taps his collar and makes a curious sound when the image appears. The caller is a grey-haired Viking male with full beard. The current picture has him offering a drinking vessel made from a horn as he seems to be shouting a toast. He has a patch over his left eye, the right is dark and sparkles with humor. The picture is replaced by a life-sized hologram of the man sitting behind a desk. He still has a patch on, leading Jesse to believe he has lost that eye. Several other men of various sizes and a couple of women also join in the call, appearing one at a time. The large man grins, cheerful to see Nako.

"Nako, we were getting worried about you," The gray-haired Viking says, his deep voice bursting from the hologram. "Has the meeting started yet?"

"Started and finished, Sir Octavius," Nako answers. "Apparently it was rescheduled to an earlier time to accommodate Senator Harry."

"Of course," the woman next to Octavius rolls her eyes. "Can you give us a brief overview of what happened?"

"Bottom line, the Ouija Software is not a viable program to release to the masses," Nako said. "I will call you back once we are at our destination tonight."

"You're not staying at the Grand Leyman?" a second man inquires.

"No," Nako, Jesse, and Louis all avow in unison.

"I will explain that when we reconvene as well," Nako assures him.

"Is it haunted?" a fourth member inquires with a snicker.

"More than haunted," Jesse answers, seriously. "It is on the verge of being cursed."

"Jesse has experienced a lot more of the ghosts than we have at the hotel," Nako said. "I promise to call you back once I am at a place where we are more comfortable."

"I look forward to the call," Octavius says. "Take care of yourselves."

"Thank you, we will," Nako said. The hologram disappears as he hangs up his phone.

"Waitress! We are ready to order!" Louis calls over to the staff. A young woman dressed in a medieval costume skips over with a grin. Nako is first to order his meal, a large tuna fish with a side of cheese. Louis orders half the menu with a large beer as Jesse orders last, pasta and a salad. The waitress walks away, and Nako sits back to watch the pageantry of the conference. Louis pulls out his small phone pad and checks his messages, reminding Jesse about her own voice mail. She takes her phone out and places a wireless earpiece in her left ear.

Jesse listens to her voice mail and arches an eyebrow before going to the video that the caller mentions. Her jaw drops when she sees a five-story robot parked just outside of her school's fence. It was not there when she left earlier in the day. Jesse tries to call her employee and does not get an answer. She dials a few others and receives the recipients' voicemails. Louis decides to send a quick text message to the people that called him.

"Don't forget the paperwork, Nako," Louis says to his friend.

"Yes," Nako straightens up and touches his collar again. A large, printed document appears on the table. "Jesse, please read the document, if you agree with the terms go ahead and sign the paperwork."

"Hmm," Jesse reads over the document. "So, the school will become a part of the museum system. I am required to host a couple of shows and special events at the college. I have room for that."

"It also says that the Museum of Past Modern History will pay for any repairs or new buildings needed to accommodate events." Nako taps the paper to point out a specific paragraph. "There is a part where the Knights of GUMA will host training sessions on the campus. If that's okay, then we can move forward."

"Do I still have control of the school?" Jesse asks.

"Yes," Nako agrees. "You will have a new title of Curator to the Museum's School of the Metaphysical Arts."

"What about my family home? It resides on the grounds," Jesse inquires.

"Everything on the grounds of the school will be under the jurisdiction of the Museum once I sign these documents. Your creditors have no choice but to relinquish the deed of your college to the Museum. It happens automatically," Nako says patiently. "If there is any intentional destruction of the school or any of its buildings, the violator will face harsh punishment to the furthest extent of the law."

"I see, any changes I make, such as renovations, have to be approved by the head curator of the museum system," Jesse finishes reading the document. "Alright, I agree."

"Excellent!" Nako does jig as Jesse signs the paperwork. He taps the hologram on a second line to include his signature.

"Congratulations Jesse," Louis chimes. "Or should I say Madam Curator."

"I just sent to you all the paperwork and your new salary as a curator," Nako informs her. "I'm very excited!"

"I'm excited because dinner's here," Louis admits as the waitress saunters over with the large cart of food.

"Thank you both," Jesse says. She feels a great weight lift off her shoulders.

The waitress flashes a merry smile as she places Jesse's food down in front of her. The new curator nods her thanks then picks up a fork to dig into her salad. The waitress leaves as a cold feeling goes down Jesse's spine. She looks up and her eyes meet those of Irava's. The strange thin woman smiles as she studies the trio.

The slow, calculated smile chills the new curator to the bones. Jesse briefly turns away from the strange woman to regather her senses. When she faces her again, there is a renewed energy within her to fight what Irava is projecting towards them. The strange woman's features seem to stretch even more as her smile brightens from the challenge.

"Is there an issue here?" a young woman inquires behind Irava.

Jesse turns her focus from Irava to the young Paranormal Investigation Unit Officer standing behind the tall thin woman. Irava whips around and stifles a swear as she backs away from the lovely young woman with dark colored hair. The officer's blue-grey eyes were not the most shocking features that Jesse takes note of. The young woman's identical double standing right next to her is what captures both Irava's and Jesse's attention. This second woman is transparent and appears to be wearing ancient clothing with a beautiful golden bow across her torso. Matching arrows are in a quiver on her back, and she seems interested in Irava's reaction. The PIU officer clears her throat to regather Irava's attention.

"Ah, no Officer Hunter. I was just admiring the restaurant," Irava says and takes another step back. "Excuse me, I have to go find my companions."

"Be sure to keep your telekinetic abilities in check while at the convention," Officer Hunter warns. "Otherwise, enjoy the events. It will be closing down in about an hour."

"Thank you," Irava says and speedily walks away.

"Hello Diana," Nako greets the officer. "I was worried about you when you didn't answer your phone. I called a few minutes ago."

"I was a little busy then, Curator Nako," Diana assures him. "A group of younger practitioners were in the middle of summoning yet another demon."

"Ah, I see," Nako pats the table. "Come and join us, I want to introduce you to Jesse Monroe, the newest member of the Museum Team."

"Ms. Monroe?" Diana says, her eyes lighting up with excitement as she sits down. "You have the Tarot Pneuma class tomorrow. My coworkers and I are looking forward to attending."

"I, unfortunately, will have to cancel the class. I will not be here to teach it tomorrow," Jesse says. "However, I will be glad to give you a demonstration."

"That will be great," Diana says as another chair scoots to the table and the second woman sits down.

Jesse explains, in brief, the history of the tarot cards as she takes her deck out of her pocket and shuffles it. She pulls out two cards, the Magician, and the High Priestess. Jesse continues her explanation by telling those paying attention to her that the cards can be used two ways. One is as the actual person represented on the card; the other is the caster taking on some of the properties of the card or lending it to others. Afterwards, Jesse holds the two cards above her head and says a couple of words then tosses them in the air.

The card of the Magician explodes over Jesse and rains dust down on her. Her clothing changes to those the figure on the card wears. The High Priestess rains down on Diana, and her PIU uniform also changes to resemble the clothing of the card. Diana looks down at her hands and clothing.

"Ok, what's happening?" Diana asks and looks up at Jesse.

"What do you feel?" Jesse asks, calmly.

"Everything has increased, all of my metaphysical and telekinetic abilities are very high," Diana answers. "Almost like when I first connected to my Aethoes, except, more controlled."

"Aethoes?" Jesse arches an eyebrow.

"I have a link to Artemis," Diana explains in brief. She glances at the archer on her left. "She said she also feels a power boost and does not feel that it is a bad thing."

"How long do the effects last, Jesse?" Louis inquires. "I'm worried about Diana."

"Let me cancel it," Jesse said.

The lights of the restaurant start to flicker as Jesse snaps her fingers. The two cards immediately reappear on the table in front of her. Diana shakes her head and places a hand upon it as she reins in her abilities. The lights stabilize as Diana exhales, shakily. Artemis pats her on the back, encouragingly. Louis keeps an eye on the officer to make sure her rate of breathing returns to normal before he finishes up his meal. Nako settles back down once the excitement is over.

"I apologize," Jesse says to the officer. "I think the enhancement of the High Priestess card and your own linkage may have been a little too much."

"I'm informed that I will be able to handle that in time," Diana said. "Can you combine cards?"

"Yes," Jesse answers. "Depending on your mystical strength, you can have anywhere from two to the entire deck, though I do not see why the entire deck would be needed at one time."

"It sounds like someone's Aethoes wants to play with Tarot Pneuma," Nako winks at the transparent woman.

"Like the Ouija board, you should not take the tarot lightly," Jesse warns. "Otherwise, I do encourage all students to have fun while learning how to wield the tarot in a unique way."

"Thank you, Ms. Monroe," Diana nods to the woman. "Speaking of Ouija, I noticed that I missed the meeting."

"It was pushed up an hour because Peter said so," Louis summarizes.

"Can you tell me what happened?" Diana asks. Her phone-orb goes off and levitates in front of her. "Wait...what?"

Diana stands up as an urgent message from Deloris comes through her phone. The officer apologizes, stepping away from the table to call her coworker. Jesse decides to finish up her meal, pleased that it is still warm, as Diana tries multiple means to contact Deloris. The young woman sits down with a frown upon her features as she contemplates her next decision.

"You could not reach Deloris either?" Nako frowns.

"What's happening?" Louis asks.

"An urgent message, call for assistance at her current location," Diana said. "This message is unlike Deloris, I'm not even sure it's from her but..."

The phone orb rings again, and this time Diana answers it. Silence greets her, causing the worry factor to increase. Jesse notices several more vendors have packed up and are leaving the convention. She finishes her meal as another urgent message for assistance flashes across Diana's phone-orb from Deloris. It does not show the location that she is requesting assistance from. Diana shows the message to her Aethoes, and both appear concerned or curious as to what is happening.

"I have to go and see what's going on," Diana says as she once again stands up. "Although it is unusual for Deloris to request backup, it's not entirely impossible."

"I've also tried to reach Deloris to no avail," Nako admits. "When you find her, let me know if she's okay. Situation pending, of course."

"Of course, Sir Sothpaw," Diana nods.

As she straightens, she fades from the area. Her Aethoes also disappears at the same time. Jesse, impressed with the teleportation spell that the young officer had employed, applaud the effort. Louis peruses the dessert menu as he chews on a toothpick. The soft whirl of the camera above them captures Nako's attention. He looks at it and notices that it is focused upon their table.

Jesse also looks at the camera and tilts her head curiously. It seems to focus in on her then the green light of the camera goes out all of the sudden as it turns off. Jesse frowns as the waitress brings over the bill. Nako pays for the meal as all three of them stand up.

"No time for dessert?" Louis asks teasingly.

"No, I think it's definitely time for us to depart," Jesse says. "I'm going to the lobby to see if my luggage has been brought as I requested."

"I've got to go to my room to pack up," Nako says as he leads the way. "It should not take long; I brought a few, simple, things."

"I'll go get my backpack from my room and meet you in the lobby, Jesse," Louis offers. "I've a friend that will take you home, no charge."

"Thank you, Louis," Jesse gives him hug. "See you in a minute."

The trio depart their separate ways, unaware of the various cameras watching their every move. In the control room, a belt loop touches a switch and the holotube changes from the interior of the hotel to a city camera facing a questionable tavern. Diana walks out of the shadows and stands in front of the door of the establishment. She frowns as she looks at her phone orb and notices that Deloris is inside of the location. Diana puts her phone away and crosses her arms, she has no desire to go into Bradly's Vampire Bar. It even has a disclaimer stating that those that enter do so at their own risk. Diana glances at her Aethoes then both take a deep breath in and open the door.

The laughter does not stop as Diana walks into the establishment and looks around. She locates Deloris immediately, sitting at the bar and watching a soccer game. She is wearing civilian clothing, her hair worn long. She is sipping on a beverage and enjoying the game. The camera on the wall focuses as Diana approaches her coworker, very aware that she is being watched by many of the patrons in the bar. Artemis gently touches Deloris on the shoulder. The vampress whips around, surprised by the visitors.

"What in the world are you doing in here, Diana?" Deloris asks, flabbergasted.

"Responding to your urgent call for backup that you sent," Diana says. "Ma'am."

"I sent?" Deloris raises an eyebrow. "I've done no such thing."

"I thought it may have been a fluke but did not want to take any chances just in case," Diana assures her as she pulls her phone out and brings up the text messages.

Deloris stares at the messages then pulls out her own phone orb and looks at the text messages. She sees that her phone somehow had sent a series of alerts and urgent texts to the entire team. A text from Rudy, another coworker, pops up informing her that he and several others are outside and asking if she is okay. Another urgent text pops up right after his message, causing Deloris to frown as she turns the phone off and stands up.

"It seems that someone has hacked into my phone," Deloris says, displeased. "Let me go make an appearance before the entire team rushes into the bar."

"That would be a great idea," Diana agrees.

Deloris turns to the door with the younger officer in tow and pauses when a large group of vampires start to surround them. Diana scans the audience and notices that a few of them appear to focus on her and are hungry. Her hand flashes as a gun appears and Artemis arms her bow. Deloris closes her eyes briefly and exhales words of calm before she meets the gaze of the grinning leader of the group. The young male vampire's smile becomes even brighter when their eyes meet.

"Step aside, Kerian. Let us pass peacefully," Deloris warns.

"Such a sweet young vixen walks into the bar, you know I can't do that, Deloris," Kerian answers.

"This is your last warning, Mr. Kerian," Diana said sternly. "Move aside."

"Such a lovely meal," Kerian stalks towards the women along with his friends. "You can't defeat all of us."

Deloris arches an eyebrow as the crowd closes in on them. The camera focuses on the situation as Kerian charges forward. The device cuts off as another belt loop pushes a button on the main computer in the hotel's control room. A ghostly chuckle fills the space.

CHAPTER FOUR

For Whom The Bell Tolls

Footsteps echo in the silent space as Jesse walks into the lobby to prepare for departure. She frowns when she notices that the entire area has fallen into twilight. All the robotic clerks have been shut down, the bellbots are all gone for the night. Jesse walks over to tests the doors and swears, they are locked tight. No one can leave or enter at this moment. Jesse makes doubly sure as she tries to figure out how the vendors in front of her departed. She makes a sound of curiosity as she goes over to the counter, and, to her surprise, they do not light up in greeting.

"Hello, can I get some assistance?" Jesse calls to the void.

"I would be happy to assist you, Ms. Monroe," Kalup answers as he walks from behind the clerks. "How can I help you, my delicate flower?"

"I want my luggage from my room and the doors unlocked so that I can leave," Jesse said.

"Not before our little arrangement," Kalup insists, a gleam in his eyes.

"My answer is no," Jesse says sharply. "I do not wish to engage in such behavior with you. Now, unlock the doors."

"Really," Kalup laughs and hops over the counter. "You think it was a request? It is something you need to do because your livelihood depends on it. I recently bought your school from your creditors."

"And Nako recently relinquished your hold on my college by signing documentation to bring it under the umbrella of the Museum of Past Modern History," Jesse informs him and brings up the documents. "Signed this evening, effective immediately."

"What?" Kalup sneers, rage overtaking his features.

"Open the door," Jesse reiterates calmly as she puts her phone away.

Kalup makes an angry sound before he grabs Jesse, pinning her on the counter. In the next instant, he is flying away from her and hits the door, cracking the glass. Jesse stands and straightens out her jacket, visibly upset at what has just happened. Purple flames erupt around Jesse's body and coagulate around her hands as she balls them into fists. Kalup uses the doors as leverage to stand up. His eyes train upon the woman that just tossed him

"You son of a bitch," Jesse says, anger in her words.

"It looks like I need to employ a different method with you, my beautiful lioness," Kalup smirks.

The hotel typhoon pulls a remote out of his pocket and hits the button. The robot behind Jesse leans forward and grabs her, much to her surprise. She hollers as it deals her a mild electric shock, breaking her concentration. Jesse shakes her head in an attempt to clear it as Kalup stalks towards her. Something whacks into the robot's arm causing it to let her go.

Kalup hesitates and looks down at the large paperweight. He sneers at the item before ducking into the darkness behind the desk. Jesse shakes off the rest of the robot's grip. She holds her head with one then both of her hands, using her fingers to gently massage her temples to clear it. Louis boldly walks over to her.

"Jesse, let me check your pulse," Louis requests. "I saw what was happening and managed to intervene just in time. Did you want me to contact the authorities?"

"Sure, right after I castrate him," Jesse says.

"I cannot allow you to do that, Jesse. You do not have the proper licenses for it," Louis jokes as he pat her on the back. "I, on the other hand, am fully license and have performed multiple castrations in my career. This will be quick, easy, and painless, at least for me."

"Deal, I'll cast a hold spell on him," Jesse said and looks around. "Of course, he disappears."

"He went through the door that is behind the last bot to the left," Louis points out. "Did you want to go after him?"

"No, I want to get at least my carryon bag and get out," Jesse reaffirms. "It has a picture of three generations of Monroe in it. Me, my mother, and my grandmother all together."

"A very important memento," Louis nods. "I'll go with you to get all of your luggage. We have to pick up Nako anyway. The old cat probably is taking a nap after all that fish he ate."

"This is not the place for that," Jesse remarks as she and Louis start at a quick walking pace back into the vendor hall. "Where are the nearest elevators?"

"Heading to them now," Louis said.

Cameras follow the duo's movements as Jesse and Louis weave through the marketplace. They reach the elevators and push the up button then wait. Jesse feels a cold wind down her spine and looks around as the doors to the elevator open. Nothing strange or supernatural happens so she and Louis board the carriage and press the button for the fifth floor. The elevator starts its journey up and passes their destination, stopping instead on the twelfth floor to let the passengers out.

The electricity to the elevator is then shut down. Louis taps a few buttons just to make sure before he and Jesse disembark the carriage. Jesse scans the area and notices that, although the gambling machines are alive and humming, no one is using them, not even the spirits of the hotel. They take a couple of steps into the foyer, noting the lack of activity and eerie silence surrounding them. The doors to the elevator slam shut. The duo turn in time to hear the entire elevator go crashing down to the first floor.

"That's not a good omen," Louis muses.

"I'm glad we got off that before it went down," Jesse expresses her relief. "But why did it take us to the twelfth floor?"

"Maybe a malfunction," Louis says then pauses when a light from under the door in front of him captures his attention. "Isn't that the room we had the meeting in?"

"It is," Jesse agrees. She jumps back when the door slowly opens on its own. "I'm not sure that's a good idea to go inside."

A strong force pushes on Jesse and Louis, causing them to involuntarily step forward. They both turn and see nothing, then are hit again, sending them into the room. The door slams shut as the hair on the back of Jesse's neck stands straight up. Light wisps of smoke fill the room from the arcane computers as they whirl and boot up. The machines go through their start up commands then immediately connect to the main internet of the hotel. Jesse and Louis face the mechanical beings as the security program launches and illuminates the middle of the room.

The holotubes on the wall display all the areas where the No-Ghost towers are located, and they appear to be blinking as new software is uploaded into their systems. Ghostly hands type in the password of the security program and the image disappears and is replaced by the somewhat cheesy introduction of the Ouija training program. The software is also being booted up by the No-Ghost towers in the locations displayed. Jesse whispers words of warning, unheard by the impromptu audience.

The screens show various patrons of the convention gawk and point at the display in awe or wonder as the hologram of the old board emerges in all locations and lazily lowers to the ground. The audible thump is louder as it repeats throughout the entire hotel. The planchette soon follows and lands on top of the over-sized Ouija boards.

"We got to get out of here," Jesse says and turns to the door.

"I tried the door several times, it's not moving," Louis agrees.

The specter, Charlie, appears to his captive audience in a brilliant red flash and grins maliciously at them. Jesse swears under her breath as she tries to figure out how the ghost reappeared from where she had sent him. Louis drops unkind words of his own when the ghost's attention turns to him. Drool drips from the specter's mouth in his excitement. The machines in the room start to hum, mimicking human voices as the sound of wood scraping against wood echoes in the hotel.

Voices on the holotubes continue to chatter as people walk to the board and touch it. Words of amazements and excitement ramp up as more and more people surround the Ouija boards. Jesse witnesses Aegis on the holotube as the Guardian walks into view of the camera. He hesitates when he sees the crowd of people admiring a strange tower that now has a giant board in front of it. He pushes through the mob to get a good look at the object.

"What devilry is this?" Aegis questions before the camera watching him goes blank.

"Those words could not be truer," Jesse responds in the room.

Cheers sound in the halls as the people yell out the letters and numbers that the planchette scrapes over to. The energy level in the hotel rises to a fever pitch, affecting some of Jesse's senses. She shakes her head in an effort not to pass out and once again tries the door. Louis's jaw drops open when several ghosts from various eras appear one by one. Each is deadlier than the next.

A strong electrical current slap into Jesse, knocking her back towards the ghosts. She lands a few feet away dazed. Louis curses as he promptly retrieves his friend and brings her back to the safe zone. Charlie lets out a squeal of glee, then maniacal laughter as portals open in all the locations on the screen where there are No-Ghost towers.

Convention patrons cheer their effort as several specters lumber out of the openings. A large amount of them the cheers start going quiet as some of them realize that the ghost they are looking at may not be friendly. In the hall, Aegis swears and orders everybody to start finding a way to exit the hotel. Many obey his orders, yet, a select few approach the ghosts in order to get a better look at them.

Some of the ghosts are trussed up in straitjackets as others are strapped into masks specifically designed to hold their heads in place or prevent them from biting their minders. A couple of the wraths, strangely enough, have sharp objects and weapons attached in place of their limbs. Many, if not all, have filed-down teeth to resemble animal-like fangs and are elongated, dripping with strange liquid.

"Sanatorium patients," Louis identifies the ghosts in the room and beyond. "Mad, mutilated.... dead.... Oh boy, we are in trouble."

"Can you break the damn door down, Aligon?" Jesse insists, more so than inquires.

A high-pitched piercing sound washes over the entire hotel, knocking a few of the patrons to their knees as it nearly blows out their eardrums. The poltergeists all over the establishment yowl in murderous glee and, en masse, rush forward. They begin to slaughter any and every living being in their way. Jesse drops unclean words when the ghosts charge towards her and Louis. She erects an arcane shield around them immediately and holds fast; the ghosts slam into it at first, then go around and through the wall behind them to escape into the main passageways. To the duo's dismay, Charlie is still in the room.

The sounds of victims as well as the sights of their untimely deaths on the holotubes fill the entire structure. Aegis appears on more than one screen within seconds of each other as he battles to save as many people as he can. All the holotubes shut down, leaving the pale glow of Charlie in the room. The ghost looks around as if searching for something.

Jesse lowers her shield as the ghost ignores them and goes over to a blank wall. The partition rises to reveal modern computers, complete with holographic terminals. Charlie uses his belts to activate the machines and begins to manipulate it with some of the same characters that Ronan had used earlier in the day. The ghost lets out a sound of mad glee as he breaks into the security mainframe, pausing for a moment to look over his shoulder at the two living beings.

Charlie's face stretches beyond that of a human as he grins at them, then dissipates as he flows into the machine. Louis shakes himself out of his stupor and turns to rapidly punch at the door and keypad, regardless of the electric shock he receives from his effort. A dragon-like growl and steam emit from him as he takes three steps back and runs toward the door, ramming it and sending himself and the door to the floor and into the hall.

"We need to grab Nako and get the hell out of here," Jesse says. She helps Louis back to his feet.

"I second that opinion," Louis agrees.

The two beat a rapid retreat to the elevators then hesitate when they see the one that had crashed is intact. The doors open with unnerving speed to allow steam to fill the halls. Strange mechanical laughter precedes the exit of three large security bots. Red dots light up onto the chest of the two living beings as Louis realizes what is happening and grabs Jesse. He yanks her to the side and around the corner from the elevator at breakneck speed as the robots unload their weapons, destroying the gambling machines.

Jesse and Louis decide to run down the hallway, avoiding the robots and elevators, to find another path down to the fifth floor. Louis glances back to make sure Jesse is keeping up with him and does not see the service cart in his path. He collides with it, causing dishes to clank and rattle, yet he is swift enough to catch the stoneware plates before they all fall. Unfortunately, at least three large platters make it to the floor. Jesse trips over one of the fallen dishes and hits the ground, swearing. She grabs her ankle as Louis repositions the plates back on the cart.

"Are you alright?" Louis asks.

"My ankle," Jesse starts, until she hears the unmistakable whirl of a security bot. "I'll get over it."

A security bot rounds the corner as Jesse gets to her feet. Strange gibberish and laughter exit its speakers as it brings its weapons to bear on the Aligon first. Louis picks up a plates and spins it on his finger. He then grabs the plate and whips around like an Olympiad discus thrower, launching it towards the bot with a grunt. The dish makes a high-pitched sound as it slices through the air. A split second later, the dish buries deep into the chest of the robot, destroying the internal circuitry and sending the security bot crashing to the floor, dead.

"Can you still walk?" Louis focuses on Jesse.

"I can run on this ankle if I have to," Jesse said. "Where are the nearest stairs?"

"Down this way, I hope," Louis offers as he picks up another plate.

The resonating gong of a magnificent church bell fill the galleries, drowning out any hope of conversation between Jesse and Louis as they trek down the hall. They pause and look around, noting that the noise is not coming from the speakers but from literally everywhere. Jesse's mind races as she tries to figure out the source until it clicks. The bells of the church are ringing. Louis tugs onto the woman to quicken the pace when he sees the second set of elevators in sight. Jesse skips trying to summon the elevators and goes for the staircase. Louis follows closely behind.

The bells resound through the entire hotel, the vibrations of which dissipate some of the lesser spirits into thin air. Aegis pauses in his activity when he hears the sound. He blocks the blade of a ghost and takes off the head, sending it back to the underworld. A few patrons of the convention also battle the ghosts to give those without metaphysical capabilities time to escape. Aegis unleashes a strong net of lightning, casting it out into the hall and destroying any attacking spirit for several yards in that direction.

"Your way is clear, find the exit before more of these abominations appear," Aegis scolds those that battle with him. "Get as many people out with you as you can."

"Where are you going, Guardian?" a man inquires.

"I'm going to find Jesse," Aegis says and disappears.

Shouts of surprise and screams of pain echo throughout the entire hotel as the door to the fifth-floor stairs slam open. Louis is the first to exit with Jesse following right behind him. The church bell continues to ring, filling the air with urgency. The duo gets halfway to their destination when they slide to a stop. People are running in a panic as they try to get as far away from the giant Ouija board and the ghost that it is bringing forth as possible. Jesse scans the area and finds the No-Ghost tower standing ominously a few feet from the board, the lights blinking madly as it continues to bring in poltergeists from various parts of the hotel.

Jesse focuses on the tower as lavender lights wrap around her body. She lets out a yell as she unleashes a bolt straight at the eye of the edifice. The No-Ghost tower explodes from the impact and the Ouija board disappears from the area. The ghosts, however, are still around. Jesse reaches into her pocket and pulls out the tarot card of Judgement, then covers her eyes along with Louis when a bright green light fills the area. The illumination fades enough for Jesse to see Christine calm her abilities and toss her hair as she glares down the hall.

"Who the hell activated that piece of crap software?" Christine demands of those still living.

"No one here. It was Charlie," Jesse answers, causing the woman to turn and face her.

"I thought you banished him," Christine demands. "How the hell did he escape?"

"I decided to figure that out once we are out of this place," Jesse responds. "Right now, we need for you to call for backup. What you see here is happening everywhere and there is no way to stop it."

"You're joking, right?" Christine snorts in distaste. "I'm not calling in on my vacation. Where is Diana? Maybe you can find her, and she can call in the rest of the PIU."

"Diana had to leave because of an urgent message," Louis answers.

"You might not like it, Christine, but your vacation is over," Jesse adds.

"You are mistaken," Christine said in a huff. "I am not hanging around here any longer. I am getting out of this hellhole."

Christine pushes past Jesse and Louis to head down the hall to the elevator shaft. The tolling of the bells seems to prompt the rest of the survivors to speedily trail after the PIU officer. Jesse counts to ten as she regains some calm. Electricity courses through the floor and rams into the elevators, illuminating them enough to see from afar. The sound of the elevators dinging and doors opening is heard. Seconds later people are once again screaming as security bots unleash a volley of bullets upon the unsuspecting crowd. Jesse and Louis run stealthily down the hall in order to avoid the robots and to get to Nako, fast.

The floor rumbles as the large, heavy, machinery charges down the passageway. Louis and Jesse duck around a corner and stay quiet, allowing the security bots to pass. Mechanical laughter echoes from the speakers of the bots, audible above the tolling bell. Jesse glances up and down the hall then makes her way to Nako's room, careful to avoid detection from the sentries. The entire hall seems dead silent, now devoid of all life. Jesse ignores the wandering souls of those lost as she continues to her destination. Once she passes them, the spirits are sucked up into a strange void with barely a peep.

The living duo reach their destination and Jesse reaches for the door. She hesitates when a blood-curdling scream from the other side echoes out. Louis forces the door open to Nako's room with Jesse close behind. A large number of bellbots swarm the entire room, bumping into each other, and seem to be seeking out the feline. Louis shouts the curator's name, bringing attention to himself. The bellbots rapidly organize and charge towards the newcomers.

Louis unleashes another stoneware plate in a similar manner as he had delt with the security bot. The fast-moving dish slices through three of the bots before slamming into the wall. a flash erupts around Jesse's form as she slams a fist to the floor. A bolt of electricity travels the short distance between her and the last of the bellbots. The electric bolt travels up the mechanical beings and shorts them out. Blue wisps of smoke drift from the bots before they fall to the ground.

"Nako?" Jesse calls above the tolling bell. Her features twist to reflect her concern when she does not get an answer.

A light goes on in the bathroom, catching her attention. Jesse, with a great deal of caution, approaches the room as Louis canvases the main sleeping area. Their footsteps are silent against the plush blue carpet, aiding in avoiding detection from the passing robotic staff in the hall. A quick glance at the cat furniture confirms that Nako is not hiding among the niches. Jesse hesitates at the bathroom when the light pops off. She reaches in and hits the switch; nothing happens. Jesse frowns, it is as if the electric has been cut off.

Jesse turns in order to help Louis with searching the main room when she feels a strange warmth upon her shoulders. Alert now, Jesse returns her attention back to the bathroom. A red glow pulsates and intensifies as Jesse wanders closer. She steps into the bathroom as the glow intensifies, lighting the entire space. The smell of blood permeates Jesse's senses as letters paint a dire message onto the wall.

"You are going to die," Jesse reads the message out loud.

The bell's tone takes on a forlorn sound as ghosts leap from the wall. Jesse curses and jumps back, barely being missed by the long claws from one of two specters. The ghost of the nurse grins maliciously at the living woman. She is not alone this time but has a large male ghost with her. He is wearing a collar, the leash of which is being controlled by the nurse.

The male is muzzled with a straitjacket on, yet the belts are loosened. They swirl around like snakes, his arms now much longer than normal. In place of his hands, he has two sharp blades on each wrist. They tap the ground in anticipation as he strains against the leash. Blood soaks his jacket as the fluid pours from the collar around his neck. Jesse erects her shield and uses a spell to push herself backwards as the ghosts attack again. She slides to a stop, catching a glimpse of Louis. She hears him as he sees the ghosts pursuing her.

"Alright, now that I have room, come on with it!" Jesse challenges as she shifts her footing to prepare for a fight.

Purple light swirls and explodes to life around Jesse, condensing into her hands at a rapid pace as the ghosts stalk ever nearer. The nurse cackles and shrieks as she removes the muzzle of the male and drops the leash. He rears up and roars, sharp teeth dripping with an unidentifiable liquid as he leaps at his latest victim. He swings his blades with intent to slice his victim in multiple pieces. Instead, they shatter against an invisible barrier. He draws back and stops in mid-shriek when he finds out he cannot move freely. Jesse lifts her hand, pushing the apparition away, and draws various symbols with the other hand into the air.

The ruins continue to burn bright purple as she moves on with her sentence. The tangle of symbols stretches out and surrounds the male ghost. A howl of disbelief exits his mouth as his body shrinks then dissipates into nothing but blue smoke. Jesse turns her attention to the nurse ghost as the specter cackles and disappears. Jesse relaxes then hastily turns to block the blows from the invisible ghost from several different angles. Flashes of purple and white indicate the direct contact of the attacking poltergeist. Jesse appears to hold something in one hand as she uses the other, glowing, to backhand the invisible woman.

The nurse reappears as her rump hits the floor. The ghost shudders, throws a temper tantrum, then gets to her feet to retreat to the nearest wall. Jesse pursues the ghost, stopping short of colliding with the wall when her prey goes through it. She glares at the barrier to try and draw the ghost back out but is not successful. Jesse swears as she slams a fist into the wall then kicks it in agitation.

"Get back here, bitch!" Jesse commands as she once again punches the wall.

"Easy girl, let's not draw any attention from the security bots pacing in the halls," Louis warns.

"Alright," Jesse reluctantly agrees. "Let's find Nako and get out of here."

The bell continues to toll as Jesse starts searching many of the other rooms of the suite. She picks up several orange pillows to make sure that the seraph cat is not masquerading as a piece of furniture. Louis looks under the various couches then jumps when his sensitive hearing picks up screaming from various victims within the hotel.

Jesse pauses in her search to look out the door, calculating how close the noise is. She shakes her head and picks up the pace as they search. She pauses when she detects a pair of feline eyes glowing from under the bed. Louis follows the woman's line of sight and peeks under the bed. A cat's paw swipes at the doctor's nose. Louis yelps and jumps in surprise as he draws back, holding the offended appendage.

"Don't scare me like that!" Nako scolds as he peeks from under his hiding place. "What in the world happened? All the robots went crazy as they were packing me up. I hear people screaming and gunfire. Then there's that church bell. I know for fact that the church downstairs does not have a mechanical system or even electricity."

"Slow down, Nako," Louis advises. "You're hyperventilating."

"Not yet, give me some time," Nako corrects him.

"Charlie has returned and used the Ouija software as well as the No-Ghost towers to bring forth a whole lot of his friends," Jesse explains.

"He also got into the computer, literally, and seems to have taken over the security program," Louis adds. "We have to find a way to contact the PIU."

"Unfortunately, the robots destroyed my collar," Nako sits and wraps his tail around his body. "Did you happen to find Christine?"

"She made it very clear she wants nothing to do with ruining her vacation," Jesse recalls.

"She does realize that her vacation was over as soon as this hell broke loose?" Nako says, agitated from the information.

"I informed her of that," Jesse agrees.

"We are on the fifth floor, right? Maybe we can escape through the window," Louis walks over to the portal. "I'd hate to try and avoid both robots and ghosts as we make a mad dash to the door."

"I agree. I'll come back later for my belongings," Nako says and walks to the window, hopping up on the windowsill.

"My room is right next door; I'll just be a moment. I want to get my memento at least," Jesse says and moves toward the door as Louis opens the window.

"Um, you might want to take a look before you leave," Louis said, his voice full of worry.

Jesse pauses then goes to stand behind her friend. Her mouth drops open as she then walks until she is at his side behind Nako. Red clouds surround the entire hotel with various spirits floating within them. Some of the clouds form faces of people laughing or screaming in pain, all appear to be crazed. Strange demon creatures fly about, capturing a few recently departed souls and consuming them. The predators appear to be made of three separate beasts, each more unique than the other. All are twisted or mutilated in some fashion. The faster predators seem to once have been women, but their arms replaced by stringy wings and hair made of tentacles or snakes. Their mouths are permanently open as a wide-eyed look of insanity covers their faces for all eternity.

Jesse braces herself on the window seal then leans to peek out the window and looks up then down, the clouds block out the sky and cover any dangers that may lurk below. A series of white lights flash upon the thick veil from below. Jesse picks Nako up and back away from the window as Louis closes it. She puts the seraph cat down and draws a strong protective seal upon the dust of the glass before turning away from the window with Louis. Unfortunately, the actions had not gone unnoticed.

"It looks like Charlie has punched a hole in the veil," Jesse says. "I'm not sure if he placed us inside it or has wrapped it around us like an extremely uncomfortable blanket."

"It looks like we have to go through the hotel to get out after all, or find a safe place," Nako says.

"Any safe places in this hotel will be temporary," Louis warns. "We need out."

"I concur with the doctor." Jesse says. "I say we make a beeline to the front door."

"Then what are we waiting for?" Nako asks and turns to face his friends. His wings and fur both stand on end when he sees trouble. "J-Jesse, L-Louis, look behind you."

Jesse whips around and swears when she sees the window bulging towards them. The glass with the symbol she has drawn is red hot. The rune itself erupts into flames. Louis turns just as the glass shatters; molten shards falling to the floor missing the witnesses. Jesse gawks and takes a step back with her friends as the three Nightmares stalk towards them.

Each stand ten feet tall or greater with three heads upon terribly twisted bodies. The first head is a human with extended eyes and drooling jaws. The middle head protrudes through the chest and resembled a mange-covered rodent with chewed-up ears. The incisors point straight out like spears. The final head is where the groin would usually be located and takes the shape of a maddened dog, complete with foam drooling from its non-existent lips.

Each monstrosity has four legs under the main body and then two additional hind legs behind to support the weight. Four arms waves from the torso along with stringy wings from their greasy backs. Jesse composes herself as she causes three tarot cards to appear in hand: The Fool, Strength, and Two of Swords.

"Nako, Louis, get ready to run," Jesse instructs her companions.

Louis reaches down and grabs Nako in a flash. He tucks the seraph cat under one arm as Jesse tosses her trio of cards at the Nightmares. Smoke erupts from the cards as the image of the Fool and his dog comes to life. He is brandishing a sword in each hand and yelling with the courage of a lion as he charges towards the Nightmares. The dog morphs into an actual lion as he attacks as well. Jesse and her friends depart the room with haste. She slams the door shut and drawing a second seal upon it.

The sound of battle within the room echoes as Jesse leads the charge down the hall. She slides to a stop and swears before pushing Louis out of the way as several bodyguard bots speed in their direction. The recognition software compromised, their eyes glow red and weapons smolder from use. Mechanized laughter echoes from them as if they drank from a well of madness. Louis curses when the bots lock on them and whip around, returning to their direction with weapons locked onto the trio. Jesse gasps when Louis passes the seraph cat to her and pulls them both along in the opposite direction of the bots as they open fire and miss.

"I'm going to see if I can get them to follow me," Louis says as they continue to run down the hall at full speed.

"What?" Jesse asks.

"Louis, be careful," Nako instructs.

"I will meet you downstairs," Louis promises.

The Aligon starts to outdistance the human woman and takes a quick turn down a small hallway. Jesse careens past the hall, sliding to stop and go back. Nako shouts at her to stop as the robots that chased them turn down the hall after Louis. Jesse pauses at the edge of the hall and stares into the darkness. She goes down into the small passageway and finds it is a dead end.

Nako turns and trembles, prompting Jesse to glance behind then press against the wall. She quiets Nako and uses her mystical abilities to fold the shadows around her, blending into the building. A set of two robots' whiz by, opening the security doors that once blocked access to the rest of the hotel. Jesse waits five minutes then releases her spell. She sets Nako on the floor as both listen. The entire floor is quiet now, with exception of the tolling bell.

"Louis could be in danger, we have to find him," Jesse said.

"Louis is a highly capable Aligon, He said he will see us downstairs, and he will," Nako appeals. "We have to concentrate on getting out of here. How long does the seal and Tarot Pneuma last?"

"The seal could last a long time, but those are Nightmares," Jesse said. "They will blast through that as soon as the cards are done, which is now."

"Wow," Nako whispers as three cards appear back in Jesse's hand, and she puts them away. "You call those demons Nightmare."

"A conglomerate of someone's bad dreams," Jesse explains as they start to walk again. "They represent madness, typically found around hospitals or sanatoriums of the past."

"Louis did mention the ghost downstairs wore hospital scrubs that he could not identify," Nako frowns. "I know a better staircase to take to the vending area, follow me."

Jesse walks next to Nako down the silent hall as they search for the staircase. The bells tolling continue to resonate as they walk, vibrating them to the core. As they pick up the pace, neither notices the creature stalking them from behind.

The bell tones reverberate, covering up the screams of the victims as Louis speeds down the hall. He jumps to avoid an errant fireball, landing and continuing his way as the spell caster meets his doom. Louis rounds a corner then pours on more speed to get some distance between himself and his pursuers. He drops an Aligon oath as he locks his legs and slide to a stop.

His sensitive hearing picks up the unmistakable sounds of more mechanical beings upon the path ahead. He whips around and sees the red LEDs flashing from the security bots that chase him growing ever nearer. Louis looks about to see that he is trapped. He turns and pauses when he sees a giant edifice full of statues dedicated to ancient anime characters. Louis hurriedly climbs the edifice, heading towards the forty-foot statue of the Monkey God.

The bots scan the area to search for a humanlike creature. Their lights flash over the statue, noting that the anime characters did not flinch or react. The light washes over the Monkey God and his small anthro-dragon sidekick standing on his shoulders. The dragon is golden and has jeans on. He has no wings, and his features remind onlookers of the mythological dragons of ancient eastern lands. Both the Monkey God and the dragon appear excited to go forth into an unknown adventure with the dragon pointing the way.

The scanning lights flash over the dragon and hesitate, detecting heatbeat. The light moves on when it does not see the figure of a human. The bots exchange information before they all head back down the hall to find more prey. the gonging of the bell barely hides the whirls of the robots' motors as they depart the area.

Several minutes will pass before the dragon shuts his mouth and looks about. His ears focus forward as he listens. When he hears and sees nothing, he jumps down from the statue. He makes sure to land as quiet as possible so that he does not draw attention to himself.

"Alright Louis let's find your friends," the dragon says to himself. He glances behind then continues down the hall, easily finding stairs that lead down.

CHAPTER FIVE

Going to Church

Shrieks of anguish from various victims fill the void between the gongs of the church bell. Jesse and Nako creep down the passageway, all while keeping a vigilant watch of where they are going. The first stairway they came across a few minutes ago are locked. Instead of forcing the stairs open, the two survivors decide to seek another way down. The fur on Nako's back rises at the same time the hair on Jesse's neck stands on end.

The two, bit by bit, turn to glance over their shoulders. To their surprise, a single light trails after them in a lazy ramble from side to side. It hesitates and bops up and down for a moment. A child's laughter emits from the light as it gets closer, alerting Jesse. She faces the light fully as it expands until it resembles the head of a deranged child. The skin is burned and bruised from a demise long ago, the eyes reflecting the same madness that seems to possess many of the ghosts encountered in the hotel, so far.

Jesse eases away from the disembodied head, keeping to the direction she and Nako are going. She listens out for whatever may come behind as she mentally shifts through her tarot deck. Nako shivers as he backs up with Jesse, staying an arm's length behind his friend. The apparition grins evilly then open its mouth. It widens several times over, allowing the top head of a Nightmare to press out. Nako emits a terrifying shriek as he turns tail and runs down the hall at full speed. Jesse swears as she takes a few steps back then pursue her companion.

The sounds of people dying increase over the bells. Jesse and Nako careen down the hall as they unknowingly head straight for a killing field. Nako turns a corner and slides to a stop from the sight. Jesse almost trips over the feline but manages to hop over him instead to avoid squashing him. Shouting in close vicinity makes Jesse focus her attention on the scene in front of her.

A large group of people are running around in circles as they attempt to flee. At least seven Nightmares as well as disembodied heads are in the center of the confused living beings, slaughtering them and consuming the souls of the dead. A cluster of bellbots make sure to keep the people from straying too far in a direction they can escape. Jesse snaps out of her shock with a shake of her head to bring herself back to her senses then glances behind. She notices that the child's head and Nightmare they had momentarily escaped from are approaching from the rear. Jesse scowls as she bends down and picks up Nako, tucking him firmly under one arm. Four cards, the Page of each suite, appear in her free hand.

"Nako, close your eyes," Jesse instructs.

"What are you doing?" Nako asks, fear ripe in his voice.

The church bell resonates as Jesse tosses the four cards. The Pages appear, each brandishing their weapon. Jesse points towards the swarm in front of them and gives an order. The Pages charge without hesitation into the fray with Jesse hot on their heels. The robots on the end are destroyed by the Pages as they cross the border. Ghosts and demons are pushed forcefully to the side, if not slain, as the warriors continue up the middle.

The living are confused but ultimately decide to follow the group. Jesse reaches the other side of the fray and continues to run as the Pages once again become cards and return to her deck. Three other living people are able to escape with Jesse. The remaining are dragged back in by unseen chains from the Nightmares in the center. Jesse and Nako do not look back as they continue down the corridor and around the corner into another elevator lobby.

"Those poor people," Nako mews sadly.

"They are caught in a web of fear and confusion," Jesse says, placing the curator back on the floor. "I tried to break it as we were going through, I thought a couple of people also made it, but I don't know where they went."

"Hopefully to find a way out without getting killed," Nako offers. "These are the main elevators that will take us down to the vendor area."

"Do you know of an alternative means to contact the PIU?" Jesse asks as she walks over to the door to the staircase.

"With this type of disturbance, I'm sure that the whole team is already here, they just have to find a way through that red cloud," Nako says.

"I don't like that cloud," Jesse says with a frown as she opens the door.

Nako's eyes widen with terror as he uses his wings to muffle a gasp. Jesse's jaw slackens from what she is witnessing. Several ghosts, dressed in surgical uniforms, are performing a lobotomy on an unwilling living victim. The woman is gagged and tied down by strange chains as the ghostly doctors proceed to pick up a used, rusty, well-tempered tool. Jesse reaches for her tarot deck.

Before she can reach it, the door slams shut. She swears as she tries to open it again and it does not budge. The victim's muffled screams are cut short as the doctors complete the procedure. The door still does not open even as Jesse punches it in anger and crouches with her head resting on her forearms.

"Jesse, we still have to continue on," Nako says kindly to the woman.

"I know," Jesse said and stands back up. "I think all the staircases are blocked."

"There is one more," Nako informs her. "Follow me."

Nako walks around a corner, pauses then immediately retreat back to Jesse's side. He informs her of the No-Ghost tower standing vigilant in the hall. Jesse frowns and peeks around the corner. The edifice is glowing strangely as the Ouija board continues to spell out various names. Something moans as chains appear on the board. Jesse swears as she sees the vague shadow of a horned beast taking shape attached to the chains.

"We have to climb down the elevator shaft," Jesse opts and adjusts her jacket while she approaches the doors. "I need my hands free so in you go."

"Normally, I would protest but with the current situation…" Nako says and hops into the jacket. He snuggles just under Jesse's bosom and stays still.

Jesse zips up her jacket only half way, taking care not to pull the curator's fur in the teeth of the fastener. She examines the doors of the elevator, doing her best to ignore the scraping of wood on wood from the Ouija board around the corner. Purple lights caress her hands as she places her fingers in the small crack. She grits her teeth and stands with her feet shoulder width apart. Using her strength and enhancing it with her mystical abilities, Jesse forces the elevator doors to open.

The sound of metal grinding against itself is barely heard above the bell yet it sounds like a beacon to the survivors. Jesse opens the doors just wide enough for her to slip in. A small ledge greets her as she hastily reaches for the cables of the elevator. The doors to the shaft shut loudly as the roar of the summoned beast echoes in the hall.

Jesse wraps her legs around the cable and descends as rapidly as she can. She reaches the top of the elevator car just as the doors above melt from an intense flame. The head of a tormented dragon appears as it looks down into the shaft. Jesse looks up and meets its gaze. She unleashes an oath her mother would not like, then quickly finds the trap door to the elevator car.

The dragon roars again and leaps into the elevator shaft as Jesse drops into the car below. She is pleased to see that the elevator doors are already open as she bolts from her location and into the marketplace. The elevator itself melts into nothing but molten metal as the dragon burns it and flies from the shaft. It lands on the floor and roars a challenge to the living woman. A deep, guttural, laugh trickles from its chest.

"Great, a dead, deranged, dragon," Jesse grumbles.

Jesse quickens her pace into the darkness of the cavernous room. The dragon lets out a sound of glee as it gives chase, tearing through the vendor booths easily. Jesse grabs a rope from a magic tricks booth and tosses it out across her path. The magical item stiffens up, as designed, and trips the galloping dragon, sending it to the floor with a grunt.

The rope then ties it up, providing the woman with a little more time to escape. Jesse hears the dragon roar as it breaks free of its bonds. As she passes yet another table, she picks up a pentagram, a deck of cards and several smoke balls. She examines her items and notices that the pentagram has a small dragon in it and the deck is a novelty set of Dragon Tarot cards.

"Never dealt with this deck before, but worth a try," Jesse said.

Jesse looks up from her bounty and swears as she slides to a stop. A giant set of iron doors now block the lobby, preventing any escape. She turns and shakes her head when she sees the dragon stalking her way. Its eyes are alight with delight from the fact that she is now trapped. Jesse takes out her new deck and sifts through the cards rapidly, coming across the King of Pentacles' dragon equivalent. She couples it with the necklace she confiscated and pulls out a smokeball as well.

The deranged dragon pauses and wiggles its backside before it pounces forward. Jesse tosses the smokeball first and creates a screen then lets the card and necklace fly. the initial flash from the smokeball startles the dragon for a moment. Undeterred, it jumps to go through the smoke with mouth agape. The deranged dragon is smacked to one side by a giant black talon.

The giant Dragon King of Pentacles roars, shaking the room and drowning out the church bell. Jesse stares at him, flabbergasted at the size of the king. Steam emits from the black dragon as the deranged dead opponent recovers and attacks again. The large dragon grabs his smaller opponent and holds him down, pushing full weight upon the creature. A squeal of pain escapes the trapped beast as Jesse takes the opportunity to flee into the vendor area.

"Nako, we have to find an alternative to the lobby doors. It looks like Charlie brought down the riot doors to block any exit," Jesse informs the cat.

"Let's get to the church to see if we can engage Aegis for some assistance," Nako suggests. "If we don't find any sanctuary, we will eventually end up dead."

"Not an option in this hotel, if I can help it," Jesse said. The card of the Dragon King of Pentacles appears in front of her. "What? Already?"

Jesse picks up and puts the card away as she passes two of the No-Ghost towers, ignoring the Ouija boards as they move to two different names. She heads to the hall that led to the church. She instinctively hesitates just within arm's reach when she notices that it is completely dark. Jesse pulls out her old Tarot deck and takes out the card of the Sun.

The ghost dragon's roar echoes in the vendor hall as the beast gallops through the area, uncaringly. Jesse turns to face the beast as a cold wind fills the area, switching her current card out for the King of Swords. The dragon leaps from the center of the room in order to devour its prey. Instead, a sword of lightning cleaves the beast in half. Jesse blinks as soft feathered wings touch her side. She stares at the back of the Guardian as he positions himself between her and the attacking beast.

"What the hell is going on?" Aegis asks, still facing the room.

"Charlie is literally bringing it to the hotel," Jesse answers. "He is using the No-Ghost towers and the Ouija software to do so."

"This monstrosity of a building is a hotel?" Aegis questions. Hissing is heard from the room causing the Guardian to frown. "Get to the church, I will talk to you about this in a moment."

Two larger creatures slither towards the pair. From the torso up, they appear to be giant cats, complete with extended claws. The rear of both beasts is the back end of snakes. The creatures' eyes are wide, their teeth and claws covered in blood. The strange abominations open their mouths as they violently hiss, their tongues resemble the head and hood of a cobra. Jesse once again swaps her cards out to The Sun and takes a couple of steps back from Aegis as the Guardian prepares for battle. She pulls shades from an interior pocket and puts them on before tossing the card into the air.

A glowing white horse appears with a brilliant golden mane. Every part of the animal is illuminated to include the flag that it has attached to its glowing saddle. It dances as Jesse grabs the reins and hauls herself onto the horse's back. She then directs it into the darkened hall and digs her heels into the horse's side.

The glowing animal rears up and bolts into the dark passageway at a full gallop. Light from the horse spreads out for several feet in front and on both sides. The rear of the animal does not shine as bright but it does travel faster than the ghosts that now give chase. Jesse holds on as the horse jumps into the air and lands nimbly on the other side of the obstacle without breaking stride. She glances back to see that her steed has cleared the head and body of a Nightmare. An obscene word escapes her as she turns back to the front, encouraging her horse to go faster.

The Nightmare's bellow of rage echoes as Jesse exits the tunnel. Her horse rears up and returns to the card, causing Jesse to land upon her backside. She gets to her feet as several security bots charge towards her. Their mechanical voices quaking with mad laughter. The open portal of the church beckons just beyond the robotic wall. The bell's gong is now ridiculously loud, shaking the foundation of the hotel. Jesse wraps an arm around the shaking Nako hiding in her jacket as she pulls out the Dragon Tarot deck. Two silver plates fly past her, whistling as they cut through the air.

The spinning disks take the heads of several robots as a golden streak follows the plates. The golden dragon takes out two more of the bots. He bends the gun of a third, causing it to destroy the interior circuitry with the backfire of the weapon. The last bot is taken out by the whip of the dragon's tail.

"Okay, I know I didn't summon you," Jesse says to the dragon as Nako peeks out of her jacket.

"Louis!" Nako announces.

"At your service," the golden anthro-dragon said and bows. "You are going the wrong way; the door is that way." He nods back down the tunnel.

"The riot doors are blocking the exit and now we can't go back that way," Jesse explains.

"I think I can get the doors open," Louis boasts as he flexes his chest muscles a little. "Why can't we go back...oh...."

Jesse turns and takes several steps back as the Nightmare she had jumped over exits from the tunnel. It is growling as it stalks towards the trio. Nako ducks back down into Jesse's jacket to hide his eyes. Jesse turns and heads toward the church. Louis follows her example, keeping close to his friends. The cavernous room yawns in front of them as the Nightmare chuckles at the runners.

The beast bellows as it crouches then launches itself into the air, landing in front of the church. Jesse swears as she slides to a stop and Louis adds to the profanity as he almost crashes into the demon. The Nightmare laughs fully as it reaches for the dragon's tail. Several flashes of light slice into the beast causing it to stiffen then fall into pieces. Each part of the Nightmare disintegrates as it hits the ground. Jesse and Louis both look to each other as if questioning the action. The Aligon is first to his feet as he helps his human friend to stand. Together they rush into the church before anything else could attack them. The bell gongs one last time then goes silent.

Brash and angry shouting replaces the loud gong of the church bell within the walls of the sanctuary. A wild-eyed man stands at the altar spewing irrational thinking while improperly quoting the Bible he holds and shakes at his impromptu congregation. His expensive tuxedo is now shredded to bits, all of his hair standing straight up on his head. His beard bushed out as though it were a frightened cat. Jesse ignores the man as she bends down and unzips her jacket.

Nako hops out of his confines and shakes off with a slight sneeze. Louis grins, showing all of his dragon teeth, his tail whips as he constructs his remarks. Jesse rolls her eyes, figuring the doctor has a naughty comment for his seraph cat friend. A whoop of joy interrupts any comments as well as the man at the podium, temporarily silencing him. Jesse stands up just in time for Christine to run over to them. Jesse dodges the blonde so that she does not get knocked over. A quick look around and Jesse also notes that Ronan has made it to the church as well.

"Nako!" Christine picks up the seraph cat much to his terror, holding him at arm's length. "Oh, I'm so glad you're still alive! This is great! Quick, you need to somehow get ahold of Deloris. My phone orb went dark a while ago."

"Unhand me, woman!" Nako demands as he wiggles, his wings splaying out as well as his legs. Christine drops the cat, causing him to fluff up.

"Why don't you try to contact her through some other means, Officer Longstraw?" Louis asks. He grins when the woman stares at him.

"Wait, you're the Aligon that was in the meeting," Christine said.

"I am," Louis nods his agreement. "You were chosen for the job at the PIU because of your extraordinary metaphysical capabilities. Perhaps you can use something to communicate with Deloris, a mirror or glass. Maybe even an Astro plane or temporary mind link."

"I'm sorry but I don't want to share any kind of connection with a vampire that has the capabilities of Deloris Matox," Christine said and crosses her arms. "I'd like to stay in control of literally every aspect of my physical and mental being."

"Fine, I'll do it," Jesse said, tired of arguing with the unreasonable woman. "Do you have a physical version of her business card?"

"No, I do not carry anything from her on my being, perhaps if I check the hall, I may find a stray card or two." Christine says, sarcastically. "Oh, silly me, there are murderous ghosts and demons all over the place. I guess we have to wait to die."

"We can also try Diana," Louis says, gently steers Jesse a distance from I haughty woman.

"True," Jesse agrees then pauses as she recalls meeting the young lady. "Wait, Diana has a link to Artemis. That might be an easier communication than reaching out in the dark to Deloris."

"So, you are going to try Diana?" Nako sits down and tilts his head curiously.

"Nope," Jesse said. "I'm going to communicate with Artemis."

"Before you do that..." Aegis says as he approaches. Many people gawk at his presence. "Can you tell me why all these demons and deranged ghosts are here? How did they get here and what is the plan to get you and the other mortals out of here?"

"I can't tell you the whys, but I did already tell you the how," Jesse reminds the Guardian. "As far as a plan to get out...."

"See!" the man at the altar shouts for all to hear. "Behold! GOD sends us his archangel to deal with YOU who deny HIS existence!"

"What manner of stupidity is this?" Aegis grumbles as he turns to face the excited man.

"He and many others in here are a part of a new radical religious group called The Faithful," Louis explains. "There is a lot of documentation about the organization. Main thing is they condemn those who have metaphysical abilities or do not believe in their faith as 'witches'."

"Angel! Use your mighty blade to send these heathens to hell as their punishment," the man at the altar commands. "Lift those whose souls are saved by your shining glory."

"I," Aegis puts his sword away, "do not understand why you would divide these survivors at their time of need."

"What?" the man blinks.

"Instead, you should be preaching for unity as you figure a way out of this hell hole," Aegis continues. "From my viewpoint, I see that if you work together will you survive this turbulent time of your life. Those creatures out there are aiming for both your blood and your soul. No amount of divine intervention will prevent them from getting it, if you do not cooperate."

"I do not understand," the man stutters.

"Let me break it down," Aegis says as he approaches the speaker. "The Spell Casters among you are going to be your salvation. They will be the ones to survive the longest against the elements beyond this sanctuary. Between you and safety."

"But...they are evil," the man whimpers.

"You need to cast aside that thought and lift the Spell Casters up to a plane higher than even me," Aegis says. "You should also pray to the Divine that their abilities do not falter as you figure out a way out of this hellish situation."

"I..." the man starts.

"I have said my peace," Aegis interrupts. "I suggest that, if you cannot change your thoughts, you should remain silent. Clear the air so that those who truly wish to save your life can have calm to think of a viable solution for all."

The silence of the church is broken by Aegis as he turns and walks back down the aisle to talk to Jesse. Christine mutters an oath under her breath then retreats to a corner as the Guardian arrives at his destination. Jesse does not notice his return as she rubs her temples in order to avoid a headache. She has cast Tarot Pneuma one to many times and needs to recharge before she does it again. Louis makes the young woman sit down before he leaves her side to approach Ronan. The programmer does not notice the dragon until he sits down next to him. Ronan stares at the six-and-a-half-foot golden creature for a long time.

"Wow, a gold dragon," Ronan said.

"Obviously," Louis agrees. "What failsafe did you build into your program in case of unlawful operation?"

"W-what?" Ronan blinks in surprise. "You are implying that my programming skills are amateurish?"

"No, it is the law that a failsafe is built in so that the program can get shut down in case it goes rouge," Louis points out. "All programs have it, what is yours since it has been hacked by Charlie?"

"Impossible!" Ronan scoffs loudly. "I am the best programmer this unworthy planet has. When I say my program is impossible to break into, I mean it."

Louis stares at the young man as if trying to comprehend the words spewing from his lips. The Aligon looks back at Jesse and notices that she is holding her head, perhaps nursing a head-ache. Nako is sitting next to her, patting her leg to reassure her. Aegis seems focused on Jesse at the moment, ignoring the stares and whispers in the space. Louis stands up, flexes, then places his thumbs in his belt loops as he turns back to the programmer.

Ronan lets out a sharp sound of surprise when he is lifted off the ground by his right leg. He looks to his ankle which is now pointing to the ceiling. The tip of a golden tail is wrapped around it. Ronan turns and shouts in surprise when he comes face to face with the mouth of the golden dragon. Louis grins, showing off perfectly pointed dragon teeth. He lifts the programmer higher so that their eyes could meet.

"Really now," Louis says in his native language. *"I know you can understand me, human, so I will ask you very clearly. I would like you to explain the impossibility to me. To the many lives that are lost because of this deranged idea of summoning and controlling things beyond the understanding of many mortals, let along humans."*

"I...I really had no choice," Ronan blurts out in the Aligon lan-guage. *"I had to do what they said. If not.... I can't say anymore."*

"What are you afraid of? Death? That's coming if we stay here and Charlie continues to manipulate the entire hotel," Louis scolds. *"What deals did you strike, Ronan?"*

The crowd inside the sanctuary begin to get restless as they witness the overly calm Aligon interrogating the programmer. Jesse contemplates for a few minutes then stands up to approach Louis and his captive. Christine backs to the door in order to leave the church and find a way out on her own. Aegis glances her way and arches an eyebrow in curiosity. The Guardian reaches for his sword as Nako jumps a good three feet in the air when the sound of a woman cackling echoes in the church.

Many of the people scream or shout prayers of repentance when the sound repeats. Jesse faces Christine as she pinpoints the noise. Louis turns his head, his tail waving a little which causes Ronan to just about loose his dinner. The sound resonates once again as Christine seems to realize it is coming from her. She hastily takes her phone orb out of her pocket and makes a gleeful sound. The item is pulsating green and red, and it vibrates as it cackles once again.

"Much as I hate to say this, but please be my coworkers," Christine whispered to herself. The phone orb lights turn solid green as it levitates just about an inch off the woman's hand. "This is Christine."

"Officer Longstraw, this is Lawson. I've been trying to reach you for a while. Glad to finally get through," a tall, muscular, older man says as his hologram appears.

"Oh, thank goodness!" Christine breathes her relief. "Are you here by yourself? Where is everybody else? This place is a bitch to handle with supernatural ability, let alone without."

"I see," Lawson frowns at the comments. His image shudders. "We are all outside. There is some sort of barrier or thick, strange-looking fog around the entire hotel. The team is working on a solution although we are a tad bit frustrated."

"They're frustrated!" Christine exclaims, interrupting her boss.

"What is your location?" Lawson asks, getting to the point.

"I'm in an old church in the middle of the hotel. Are you sending a rescue?" Christine inquires, her attitude more chipper now.

"No, I'm sending orders," Lawson corrects.

"Orders? On my vacation," Christine's lip turns up in distaste. "I don't want to deal with this crisis on my days off."

"Give me that," Jesse snatches the orb from the owner before her boss could retaliate. "Lawson, sir, I am Jesse Monroe. The situation is that there are about a hundred living people trapped in a small church that occupies a large lobby in the hotel. There may be more survivors throughout but I'm not sure. All of us are trapped by a variety of demons and ghouls. What assistance do I have to provide to assure we reach safety?"

"We have someone with good sense," Lawson said enthusiastically. "Your name sounds familiar Ms. Monroe."

"Former Chancellor of the Monroe College of Metamorphism. Now Curator of the Museum of Past Modern History's School of the Metaphysical Arts," Jesse introduces.

"That's a mouthful, however I'm glad that you are there," Lawson said. "Since Christine is now on unpaid leave until further notice, your assistance will be greatly needed."

"Wait, What?" Christine says, taken aback by the comment.

"Officer Moody will convey what we learned about the grounds this hotel stands on and you can fill in the blanks and brief us on anything we missed," Lawson says.

"I'll do my best," Jesse assures him as she sits down.

"Gather round everybody," Lawson calls to his officers.

"Hello Ms. Monroe," the hologram shifts from Lawson to a young dark-skinned man. "I'm Officer Moody. I'm starting by sending you some information."

The orb pulsates a few times as the hologram shifts to documents and a floorplan. Jesse reads the documents as she listens to the young man explain that the Leyman Hotel and Casino is built upon the ruins of Woard Asylum.

Louis sits down, lowering his captive to the ground but still keeping hold of him. The information does not bode well with the Aligon doctor. Jesse and Louis both frown when they learn that much of the stone and other items found on the site are incorporated into the hotel, to include tombstones at the base. Nako mews a swear as he lays down and focuses on the documents. Aegis tilts his head when the document that Jesse is reading switches to the floorplan. The Guardian's features darken as he recognizes the building.

"I know that place," Aegis said. "This situation has just gotten a lot worse than I originally thought."

"It gets a lot messier; I think I know the hacker that has you trapped but let me send over a few more goodies," Officer Moody said.

More documents appear in the air to include another map, a list of prisoners from the asylum, and a small list of other occupants that were upon the grounds prior to the hotel. Those include a human meat factory, an illegal orphanage that used children as experiments, and a morgue. Jesse scans those documents and closes them in favor of the list of inmates. She scans through it and stops when she sees a name that seems familiar.

The PIU officer sends over the picture when she requests it, and her mouth drops open. The two-dimensional photograph is of a handsome man with a diabolic grin. His light green eyes are full of pure madness, yet a spark of intelligence is identified within the depths. His dark hair is brushed down in spots yet forms points on the sides of his head. In the picture he is wearing a striped shirt with a name badge proudly printed in gold.

Underneath the picture, he is identified as Woard Asylum's Star Prisoner, Charlie Hular. Jesse scans the picture a couple of times then switches to his record. Charlie was a serial murderer using digital technology, rapist, gambler and above all an unstoppable cyber-criminal. Jesse once again looks at the picture and focuses on the eyes. An image of the summoned ghost seems to overlay the picture, matching it perfectly. Jesse gets to her feet in her surprise, nearly dropping the phone orb as she did.

"You've got to be kidding me," Jesse exclaims. "Charlie was a universally renowned Cyber-Hacker?"

"What?" Ronan asks. "Do you mean Charlie Hular? That's the only cyber-hacker that is universally known."

"That's him," Louis answers. "And it would explain how he got into your impossible to hack Ouija software."

"Ouija software?" Officer Moody asks. "Whose damn fool idea was that?"

"I have the programmer right here," Louis says and lifts Ronan up again. The young man swears bitterly.

"Like your gifts, Officer Moody, it goes downhill from here," Jesse informs the man. "Charlie is using the No-Ghost Inc. towers as a mechanism to run multiple copies of the Ouija board. Each is about as large as a conference table and very, very real."

"He also hacked into the security system of the hotel and who knows what else," Louis adds. "He is using the security bots as a means to slaughter as many living people as he can."

"Don't forget the bellbots," Nako speaks up. "I'm sure he's gotten into all of the systems by now."

"That son of a…" Officer Moody starts.

"Manners, L.A.," a woman says as she takes the phone orb from him. "We meet again, Ms. Monroe."

"Deloris, glad to see that you are still around," Jesse greets her with a nod. "Nako was worried about you."

"Diana and I are both alright. It turns out that my phone was indeed hacked, and we now know the culprit," Deloris said. "Diana gave me a brief on what she learned from you about the Ouija software. I know you probably figured this out long ago but in order to get you and the people to safety, you need to deactivate the program. It will stop the summoning of the spirits and other unsavory beings. However, those that are already there will still be an issue."

"We have been trying to get Ronan to tell us how to stop it," Louis said. "What about the red fog on the outside?"

"Red fog?" Aegis asks, his voice raises. He turns his attention towards Ronan as Louis once again lowers the programmer to the ground.

"You are still on Earth if that is a concern. We see the hotel, but this strange mist is blocking all of our efforts to get inside. Once you deactivate the Ouija program, we will be able to finish off what is left of the red fog," Deloris said.

"My advice, Lady Officer, is that you do not go near the mist," Aegis says as he steps closer. "Do not inhale it or touch it. To do so may start a downward spiral into the clutches of the Mistress of the Flames."

"Mistress of the Flames?" Deloris asks. "Can you elabo…." the orb goes silent.

"Damn it," Jesse shakes the orb. "Christine, how do you work this thing?"

"I'm not calling her back," Christine said. "Besides, my battery is probably dead from all the documents you received."

"Deep breaths," Jesse tells herself as she sets the orb down, deciding that arguing with the woman is not worth it. "We now have to determine how we are going to deactivate the program and robots."

Quiet sounds of hope rise from the people in the church as Jesse walks to the door and takes a look out. Nako rubs against her leg before sitting down next to her and staring into the darkness with her. Robotic security bots pace around, seeking anything alive. The ghouls from the ground's checkered history watch from a safe distance. Jesse crosses her arms as she looks past the obstacles and into the tunnel that leads to the front door. She knows the riot doors are down but perhaps she can use her new Dragon Tarot cards to open it. Aegis stands behind Jesse as he too studies the scene.

"This mission is a lot more dangerous than anything you have ever faced, Lady Monroe," Aegis said to her. "How can I be of service to you?"

"Really?" Jesse asks as she turns and face him.

"You are the only Spell Caster I see making an effort to get as many people out as you can," Aegis observes. "I want to help."

"Well," Jesse walks past him and faces the room. "First, we have to figure out a way to get Ronan to the origin, where the software was first activated. That's the twelfth-floor conference room."

"W-what? What do you mean I have to go there??" Ronan demands.

"You clearly indicated that it was impossible to remote into your software, Ronan," Nako reminds him as he sits in front of Jesse. "The other option is to take you to the room, and have you stop it there, since you are the only one who knows how to run your program."

"Great idea," Louis lifts the programmer as the young man hollers. "When do we start the journey?"

"Wait, please! There is a way! There is a way to break into the program remotely!" Ronan shouts as he waves his arms. "It has a guest account that I installed for testing. I can try to backdoor into the main program from there. I just need a computer."

"Hell, we should have thought about threatening him with that in the beginning. Saves me a few scales," Louis grins. "Since we are dealing with a renowned cyber hacker, we might want to have a computer that's not touched the network in recent weeks.

"Good luck in finding one of those," Christine snorts. "Everything, including my phone orb has touched this network."

"I didn't bring my computer. My phone has limited capabilities," Jesse scowls.

"I lost mine in the battle to get here," Louis grumbles.

"I don't have…" Nako starts. His eyes widen as his memory kicks in. "Oh! Yes, I know where one is at! It has not touched any network at all in a long time." He hops to his feet and starts doing a little dance.

"Does it still work and is it compatible with the network of today?" Louis inquires.

"Yes," Nako nods with a grin. "It is in the hotel's museum shop. Lots of trinkets are there too. They could come in handy."

"Who's going to go out into that hell hole and get the damn thing?" Christine demands.

"Not you, I'm sure," Jesse places a hand on her hip, coyly. "Why ruin your vacation, eh?"

"You…" Christine sneers.

A choir of 'not me' rings up from the masses. Jesse taps her fingers upon her bicep as a sour look crosses her features. With a deep breath, she goes back to the door to look out, ignoring the people. She stares out into the space as her mind goes over the grueling task of getting to the church to begin with. Jesse glances back and notice that many of the survivors are either the 'Faithful' or minor mages, their talents more for show than surviving an onslaught of attacking ghouls.

Louis drops his captive and unwraps his tail as he goes to stand next to Jesse. He places a hand on her shoulder, prompting the woman to look at him. At first, she sees his chest, then looks up at the six-and-a-half-foot dragon. He grins at her, causing her to return the smile. Aegis stands next to her and folds his arms as he glares into the space, understanding that whoever goes in there may not survive. He looks over at Jesse, understanding that she is possibly the most powerful Spell Caster in the sanctuary. His attention falls momentarily onto Christine. He shakes his head, the PIU officer is now sulking in a corner and unwilling to help anyone but herself. Jesse takes a deep breath in, tired of hearing the negative words of those behind her.

"Alright already," Jesse says and faces the room once more. "I'll go get the computer."

"I'll go too, you need a guide, and I am the key to get the computer out," Nako volunteers.

"Ronan, you better be ready to go when we get back," Louis says to the programmer. "The quicker you bring it down the faster we are able to get out of here."

"Thanks Louis," Jesse smiles, acknowledging the doctor's offer to volunteer.

"Hey, that's what Aligons do," Louis puffs up his chest, his tail swishing proudly. "We protect our friends, no matter how powerful they are."

"I too wish to volunteer to go," Aegis says. "However, my instinct is telling me that I will be needed here."

"We should not be too long," Jesse tells him.

"You have one hour," Aegis informs them. "Regardless of my instinct, if you are not back, I will come looking for you."

"With the number of ghosts and other demons in this place, give us a least two hours," Jesse beseeches.

"Hmm...alright...." Aegis grudgingly agrees. "I will clear your way."

The Guardian fades from sight as Jesse and her friends once again step over the threshold. The security bots notice them and start to line up, focusing their weapons on the three. A new set of bots have also joined their ranks, knife-wielding cook bots that cackle hysterically as they whirl around in place. Aegis appears, standing at the edge of the walkway, catching Nako's attention.

Thunder roars outside, muffled by the building. A lightning bolt slams down onto Aegis as he pulls his sword. He lets out a mighty yell as he swings it in a large sweep. A bright white light exits the tip and arches towards the army of mechanical beings. The lightning arc hits the first row of robots and spreads rapidly between them, shorting out the entire group in seconds.

The ghosts appear and attack. Aegis holds out his hand and speaks five ancient words. All the ghosts in the area yowl as they are drawn towards one of three tombstones in the small graveyard of the church. The last ghost, the nurse, hollers as she manages to free herself from the grip and escape down a dark tunnel. Aegis frowns after the ghoul then turns to the trio.

"Two hours," Aegis reminds them.

"Are you sure we can't take him with us?" Louis asks.

"Let's go, we don't have a long time," Jesse scolds.

She moves forward, ducks under Aegis' left wing, and continues to the tunnel. Nako jogs after her. Louis shakes the Guardian's hand then hurries after his friends. Just above the door to the tunnel, a camera whirls as it focuses in on the church. Aegis flaps his wings once before folding them down. He puts his sword away then walks into the structure. The holotube switches from the church to a distant garage on the hotel property.

Lights pop on showing a large collection of military-style robots. These bots are designed specifically for war. Each bot is one story tall with large laser cannons, two machine guns, and a large circular saw for hacking. Their heavy bodies are made from metal unknown to Earth and impervious to any attack. Tank treads remain the choice mode for the bots to transport themselves to their destination.

The LEDs on the military bots begin to flash and flicker as they are activated, and their software compromised. The LED eyes of the bots glow red as deep mechanical laughter exits from their voice boxes. One by one the diesel engines of the bots start up as they turn. They destroy the wall between the hotel and the garage, killing several people as they slowly roll through the hall towards the unsuspecting church. A belt loop hits a button to switch the cameras once again.

The camera on the light pole outside of the hotel entrance lights up and focuses. The red fog around the building has thickened considerably. Within the mist are faces in both anguish and pleasure of being part of the cloud. All the spirits within share a common madness. The camera draws back to show a small group of people outside of the hotel. The lens zooms in on a single woman within the group. The PIU uniform comes clearly into view on the young lady being watched. Diana faces the camera, a displeased look on her features. Seconds later, the camera goes black as it is destroyed.

In the military garage, half of the bots pause as they receive different orders. They do an about face and burst through the garage wall that leads outside, making their way to the front of the hotel.

CHAPTER SIX

Digital Relic

The halls echo with the screams and regretful moans of those killed within the area. Jesse watches various specters float around aimlessly in search of a way out. A few re-live their final days by falling in a place where there is a pile of blood or body parts. Nako makes a decision to ride on Louis's shoulder in order to keep his paws clean. The air thickens as thunder rumbles from within the hotel. Jesse concludes that it is a practitioner somewhere that is still alive and fighting to get out. Louis pauses when the thunder occurs again, this time accompanied by the shaking of the hall. Jesse pauses next to the Aligon, her attention on the wall a short distance in front of them.

"What's wrong?" Jesse asks.

"I hear a heavy motor," Nako warns.

"Security bot?" Jesse frowns.

"Much bigger, I hear it too," Louis confirms.

"That concerns me, as well as the fact that I don't see any of Charlie's friends," Jesse comments. The sound happens again. "Yeah, that's not thunder."

The wall in front of them explodes outward. Jesse reacts immediately by putting up a shield. The debris hits it forcefully, yet Jesse manages to keep it up. Louis drops a group of unclean words when the air clears. A robot at least a story tall and as wide as the hall centers on them. It is painted a strange camouflage color, suited for a desert environment. Tank treads maneuver the bot completely through hole it created in the wall.

The large saw blade starts to spin as the bot swings its arm around. Louis grabs Nako with his tail and Jesse under one of his arms then leaps back to avoid the spinning blades. Nako is now facing the back and cries out in surprise and fear. A large group of asylum ghosts fill the hall behind them. Jesse stares at the mechanical obstacle as she pulls out a smoke ball as well as the King of Swords from the Dragon Tarot deck. The military bot laughs as it brings it cannons to bear on the trio.

"Jesse, Louis, I don't mean to alarm you, but we now have ghosts behind us," Nako announces.

"Louis, I'm going to use a card on you," Jesse warns.

"Let 'er rip," Louis says.

Red crosshairs light up on the trio as Jesse tosses the smoke ball onto the floor, at the same time tossing the card into the air. A flash followed by smoke fill the hall as a great roar radiates from its core. The cannon on the military bot is smacked by a giant golden claw, causing it to face straight up as it fires. Debris from the floors above rain down upon the military bot, burying it.

The ghosts blocking the way to the vending hall attack. It is short lived as they are eradicated by purple flames emerging from the dragon's giant maw. The smoke clears allowing Jesse and Nako to open their eyes. They are now riding on the back of the enormous golden dragon. The beast raises his head and snorts confidently.

"Whoa," Nako looks around. "Where is Louis?"

"We are on his back," Jesse explains. She looks up when she hears a distinctive crack from above. "Louis, we have to get out of here before the ceiling collapses."

The dragon looks up with a curious sound emitting from his throat. A large fissure opens up above as he watches. The dragon looks behind to see the bot is buried and the way forward is blocked. He faces the direction they came from and charges forward at full speed. Jesse drops an unladylike swear words as she clutches onto the dragon's back. Nako digs in his claws as he holds on for dear life.

The ceiling starts to fall behind them with an enormous noise. Louis unleashes a mighty roar as he feels parts of the debris hitting the tip of his tail. He leaps and dives from the hall, back into the vendor area, reverting back to his normal dragon form at the same time. Nako lands on his feet as Jesse ungracefully lands on her rear. Louis slides to a stop, sprawled out upon his back on the floor, panting for air.

"My goodness, are you two alright?" Nako asks as he approaches his friends.

"I'm alive," Jesse says She holds her back and stand. "I will be seeing a chiropractor when we get out of here."

"I'll make it," Louis says and sits up. His tail taps the floor. "That was intense, what card was it?"

"Dragon King of Swords," Jesse answers and picks up the card next to the Aligon.

"The amount of energy and strength felt by being infused with the card," Louis pauses as he thinks. "I'm not sure if I liked it or not."

"It also takes an extraordinary amount of energy to manifest them," Jesse agrees.

"I..." Louis pauses and jumps to his feet when his hearing detects the robot's motor. "We have to move."

"Quick, this way. It leads to the kitchen," Nako says as he heads to a smaller passage.

Jesse and Louis follow Nako without hesitation. As soon as they enter the kitchen passageway, the military bot blasts through the collapsed hall. Deep, mechanical, laughter rolls from its speakers as it scans the room for any signs of life. It detects the hall that the trio ran down and heads after them. Before it reaches the passageway, it pauses as it receives another set of orders. The bot reverses and drives to the hall that leads to the church, turning and standing guard to wait for their return.

The smell of food and kitchen trash fills the space and is a change from the strong odor of the dead. The blend, though nauseating, did not deter the trio as they walk in silence. The passage is surprisingly well lit compared to the rest of the hotel. Jesse takes the opportunity to relocate the Dragon Tarot Card deck from her jacket to her back pocket. Louis stretches and rotates his limbs as they follow the seraph cat.

"Jesse, I thought your Tarot Pneuma lasted longer than what we witnessed against the bot," Nako said conversationally.

"It usually does," Jesse agrees. "There are two factors that is limiting the length of my abilities. One is that the Dragon deck is new, I've never worked with it before. The most prominent thing though is that I am fatigued from this entire ordeal."

"Are you on the cusp of burning?" Louis asks, concerned.

"Not yet, and that's why I put the Dragon deck up," Jesse said. "I saw what happened to my mother when she started to burn, I don't want that to happen to me."

"Did she survive?" Louis asks.

"She did, for about six months, then succumbed to her injuries," Jesse recalls, her voice saddened. "I recently lost my grandmother. She joined my mother about a week before this convention. The only one left besides myself is my grandmother's cat, Aggie."

"Oh, Jesse I'm so sorry," Nako pauses and sits down in front of the woman. "How old was your grandmother?"

"Well past one hundred, I think," Jesse answers honestly. "I never asked."

"My condolences, Jesse," Louis says meaningfully. "We can never replace our loved ones, but Nako can be a good stand in for a grandpa, he's near one hundred at least."

"Oh hush, you're at least old enough to be her pappa," Nako scoffs as he turns, tail in the air, and continues on his way.

"I... think I like that idea," Louis said after careful consideration. "So, Jesse. From now on, anyone that wants to date you has to pass through my stringent tests before they can. Of course, they have to have you home prior to sundown."

"I don't think being adopted by an Aligon is a bad thing," Jesse said, humored by the antics. "Will you be using the dragon form for intimidation?"

"Of course, it would not benefit me if I did not," Louis puffs out his muscular chest.

Louis does a little strutting as he follows the seraph cat. Jesse laughs as she shakes her head, increasing her pace to catch up with Nako. Louis grins as he changes his gait to a normal walk and easily pulls alongside the two. The swinging doors to the kitchen open as the trio walk into the space. The entire room is full of meals that are prepared for guests but will never be delivered.

The meals go from tempting to outright foul as Nako leads the way through the kitchen to the dining room. Jesse looks around then stops in her tracks and takes a sharp breath in when she sees the severed head of a human staring back at her. She shuts her eyes and bites back her immediate reaction to scream. Louis takes her hand and guides her past the grotesque obstacle.

"Why do you think military bots are at this hotel?" Louis asks to distract his friend from the scene.

"Kalup's company has a hand in a lot of things," Nako answers. "I'd have to look it up on the network to see exactly how extended he is."

"After this incident, his constituencies may start pulling their contracts," Jesse predicts.

"If he's dead, they might be void anyway," Nako remarks. "I don't think he has heirs."

"That he will claim," Jesse adds. "I'm sure I'm not the first woman he's written his demands to in a not-so-discrete letter."

"You may be the last, though," Nako said.

"What letter? I missed a letter?" Louis frowns.

"We'll talk when we get out of here, Louis," Jesse promises. "How far is the gift shop from the dining room, Nako?"

"Not very far to the entrance, it's just up the hall," Nako says, cheerfully. "It is the same door we went to earlier in the evening, Jesse."

The swing doors leading to the grand ballroom-turned-dining room open into the room. The trio push past the threshold and pause. The hardwood floors have splashes of different-colored blood decorating it in a morbid painting. The heads of humans and other universal beings hang from meat hooks and chains that dangle from the ceiling. The bodies of the victims are strewn across the many tables, being butchered into choice cuts of meat by several strange-looking ghouls.

They are hunchbacked, with green skin and dragon-like tails. Their hands are either talons or replaced with meat cleavers. Larger versions of the ghouls hack off huge chunks of various corpses and send them through a different door to the kitchen via a headless bell-bot. Chairs are bonded together with strangely glowing goop, creating a prison for the last living victim of the monstrosities. Jesse recognizes Kalup Leyman and crosses her arms in contemplation. Louis looks around and also spots the prisoner.

"That's Kalup, right?" Louis inquires in a hush tone.

"It is," Jesse answers in a hush tone.

"Should we rescue him?" Louis continues.

"I'm thinking about it," Both Jesse and Nako answers at the same time.

The hair on Jesse's neck raises up, alerting her to familiar danger. She glances around the room, spotting the nurse ghost walks through a wall into the room. Nako sees the ghost and hurries to the exit. Jesse swears internally as the seraph cat's movements capture the attention of the nurse ghost. The specter turns, spots Jesse, and starts hollering an alert. The butcher ghosts turn and yell to express their displeasure at the uncaged living. Kalup stands up and looks at Jesse as she sifts through her Tarot deck. She takes out two cards, the Aces of Swords and Staff.

"H-Hey!" Kalup waves his arms. "Help! Don't leave me!"

"Staff or sword?" Jesse inquires of Louis.

"Staff preferred," Louis answers.

Jesse tosses her two cards into the air as more butcher ghosts appear and move to the attack. The cards explode as they morph into the weapons of choice. Jesse grabs the handle of the blade as Louis takes hold of the staff. They charge towards the ghosts, momentarily stunning them. Jesse uses her sword to take the heads of at least two of the ghosts, causing them to disappear as soon as they are defeated. Louis uses the staff and delivers a blow strong enough to break his attacker in half. The ghost dissipates from the room. Jesse centers on the screaming nurse ghost and goes after her with speed and purpose. The shrieking nurse screams even higher as she rapidly flees through another wall. Jesse swears at her luck as Louis takes care of the rest of the butcher ghosts.

"She'll be back with reinforcements," Louis observes.

"I know," Jesse grumbles as she walks over to the cage containing the hotel tycoon. "I suggest you duck, Mr. Leyman."

Jesse swings the sword back as Kalup's face lights up with joy. His joy turns to horror when he notices the blade gleaming in the light. He has little time to swear and duck as Jesse swings the sword around. The wood shatters on the chair cage, allowing the prisoner to escape. Jesse gives Kalup a single look immediately heads to the exit. Louis trails after her with Kalup taking up the rear. The nurse ghost returns with reinforcements. A group of Nightmares and asylum ghosts utter various cries as they go after the living. Jesse enters the hall first and swears when she sees a No-Ghost tower sitting just a few feet from the door. The planchette starts to move at a rapid pace.

"Jesse, no time to stare at this thing. Let's get going, she's back and she has friends," Louis says of the nurse ghost as he tugs on Jesse's arm.

Kalup exits the dining room and rushes after Jesse and Louis. He catches up to them seconds before a Nightmare burst through the doors of the dining room into the hall. It rears up and bellows in preparation for a great leap to cut off the living. Instead, the demon is smashed by a large claw. The emerging creature then eats the Nightmare as it solidifies from the Ouija board. Two cat-snake beasts shriek with mad glee as they run after Jesse and Louis.

"Jesse! Louis! This way!" Nako calls from up the hall.

Kalup almost tramples his rescuer as he heads to the gift shop, following Nako's voice. Jesse and Louis keep pace with each other until Jesse turns to face her attackers. The ghosts howl in glee until she casts a banishment spell, sending the first wave back to their afterlife. Unfortunately, more take the place of the banished. Jesse sneers then turns to run down the hall. She takes three steps before her ankle rolls, sending her to the floor in pain. She gasps when she is wrapped by the golden tail of the Aligon and lifted off the floor.

Louis increases his pace and passes Kalup as he skates around the corner, jumps over Nako, and dives into the giftshop. He makes sure to keep Jesse elevated so that she does not get hurt during the jaunt. Nako follows his friends in without hesitation. Kalup is last to dive and roll into the gift shop, barely being missed by the ghosts. Large glass doors instantly close behind him. Jesse is lowered to her feet as the ghouls beat upon a mystical shield.

"You are not shielding us, are you Jesse?" Louis inquires.

"I didn't have time," Jesse said.

"If you're not then who is?" Kalup demands.

The specters growl and spit as Jesse gradually approaches the glass door. Every time they slam or claw at the glass, the barrier lights up in gold. She studies the spirits, noting that many of them are recent additions, somehow maddened to join the asylum ghouls. The half cat and half snake demons rear up and try to use their body weight to break the glass to no avail, it lights up and keeps them out.

Jesse notices several Egyptian symbols light up on the metal areas around the glass with every blow. She turns and looks around then up to see a giant black cat statue grinning back at her. The statue appears to be carved out of a single stone and anatomically correct for the species. The name is inlayed with gold upon a collar around the neck. Golden earrings grace the ears of the cat with a gold ring pierced through the nose. More gold paint outlines the eyes that glow with powers from another world. Many of the symbols upon the statue's body also flash every once in a while, when the barrier is hit.

"I believe she is doing it," Jesse nods to the statue.

"Who?" Nako turns. "Bastet? Do you have a link with Bastet like Diana does to Artemis, Jesse?"

"Oh, no," Jesse said. "I don't have a link like that and not sure if I want one."

High pitch screaming as well as her friend's surprise reaction pulls Jesse's attention back to the glass doors behind her. The cat-snakes are now attacking the ghosts and spirits that once pursued the living group. A cluster of Nightmares try to escape the more powerful demons. Unluckily for them, they are grabbed by the apprehensive tail of the largest cat snake and eaten. The rest of the spirits suffer the same fate as a feast for the more powerful demons. The nurse ghost once again manages to escape from the fray as the last of the pursuers are eaten by the cat demons. The cat demons hiss and snicker as they then turn invisible.

"It looks like they are trying to lay a trap for us," Jesse observes. She once again faces her companions and limps toward them. "We have to find another way out or a way to get through them."

"The other way out was the museum's main entrance. That has been destroyed by the military bot," Nako informs her.

"Before we figure another way, you have to recover some of your energies, Curator Monroe," Louis said. "We are going to take a little trip to the snack aisle."

"That's where I'm heading," Jesse agrees.

"I'm going to take a look at that ankle as well just in case we have to run. I don't want you to damage yourself more than you already have," Louis said.

"Wait, we are leaving here? Why? We have protection and provisions," Kalup said. "Why would we even go back into that madness? Can't we stay here until the rescue units come?"

"Because they can't get in and we can't get out as long as Charlie has the Ouija program and robots under his command," Jesse informs.

"Charlie? The ghost? I thought you banished him," Kalup frowns.

"So did I," Jesse said as she limps away. She keeps her swearing to herself as Louis once again lifts her with his tail.

"No need to do more damage than what is done," Louis scolds as he carries her deeper into the store.

"I will go find some bandages just in case she needs a splint, Louis," Nako offers as he heads in a different direction. Kalup frowns and decides to follow the Aligon.

The snack aisle is full of favorite junk food as well as a few unknowns. Jesse figures that it is stocked this way for the now-debunked convention. There were practitioners from all over the known universe that are now spirits wandering the halls. Jesse picks up a favorite peanut butter energy bar then gingerly walks over to a chair and sits down. She nibbles on the bar as she takes out the Dragon Tarot deck and begins studying them one at a time. Louis looks at the bar then goes over to the Aligon section of the snack aisle and places his hands upon his hip. He picks up a bar, reads the ingredients, then nods and joins his friend.

"Jesse, let me take a look at that ankle," Louis said as he places the bar in her lap.

"It's tender," Jesse warns then looks at the bar. "What's this?"

"It's an Aligon 'Mystic Recovery' bar," Louis explains. "It will help you regain your metaphysical strength faster than just the peanut butter bar you just got finished consuming. Also, it is more filling."

"Thank you, Dr. Lygtbut," Jesse replies, graciously.

Jesse unwraps her new snack then grits her teeth as Louis, with great care, removes her shoe. Nako bats a box containing an ankle wrap into the area. The seraph cat smacks it again, and giggles as he pounces on it. Jesse smiles at the antics as Louis, using a great deal of care, moves the swollen foot in a couple of directions. He notices that the ball of the ankle is at least three times bigger than it should be.

Nako makes a sad sound when Louis picks up the box. The seraph cat then decides to head into the darkness of the gift shop in search of the item they've come for. A short distance away, Kalup glares with seething rage at the Aligon, bitter with how close Louis is to the object he desires. Louis ignores the vibes from the human as he finishes wrapping Jesse's foot and puts her shoe back on.

"Well, unfortunately it looks like you damaged your Achilles tendon," Louis informs as he looks up at her. "You are going to have to walk, so I stabilized it as much as I could."

"What if I have to run?" Jesse questions. "We've been doing a lot of that lately."

"If we have to run, I will use my tail to carry you," Louis says. "I'm a constrictor so I know that having that wrapped around you is uncomfortable. I limit the squeeze for my friends."

"I appreciate that," Jesse finishes off her bar. "Where did Nako go?"

"He wandered off," Kalup says as he draws near. "You should not trust the Aligon so quickly. Those ghouls that held me captive were once Aligon butchers. They specialize in processing humans into meat and other products."

"Although I acknowledge that my kin have a dark past here on Earth, it is nothing compared to the history of humans as a whole," Louis says and stands. "Jesse has nothing to worry about, I assured that the ingredients of the bar she has are all plant based. I would not willingly subject any of my friends to something so vile as human meat products. I don't even eat it myself."

"I trust Louis," Jesse informs and stands. "I don't trust you, Kalup."

"Ready to go?" Louis grins, his tail waving in anticipation.

"I am ready to get the hell out of here," Jesse corrects him. "The sooner we get that computer, the sooner my dream will be realized."

"I still think it is a mistake to leave here," Kalup said.

"Then you can stay by yourself. I'll make sure they send someone to retrieve your body," Jesse informs him and walks into the twilight of the gift shop in search of Nako.

"Charlie has taken over every known network within this hotel, Kalup," Louis informs him. "I'm sure he has branched out into the ones connected to it as well. Especially if this monstrosity of a hotel is any kind of information hub."

"I don't believe you, lizard boy," Kalup sneers his insults.

"That's your downfall, hairless monkey boy," Louis shrugs. He leaves the hotel tycoon in search of his friends.

The eerie glow of emergency lights illuminates the museum area that Jesse finds herself perusing in search of the seraph cat. Shadows seem to dance with the flickering bulbs, giving the illusion of people walking. Ancient electronics encased in glass shells sit silently as she walks past. The paintings displayed of their inventor stare at the woman as if in detest. Jesse pauses when she hears Louis walking behind her. She waits for him to catch up before they both continue into the Museum of Technology. Both are aware that Kalup has followed them.

"I don't think Charlie can use any of this technology, which is a good thing," Louis muses.

"My question is, can we use what is in this place?" Jesse points out.

"I hope so, else Nako has got some explaining to do," Louis said.

"Louis! Jesse, over here!" Nako meows loudly. "I found it!"

"Promising?" Louis inquires.

Jesse gives a single look of doubt before she heads towards the seraph cat. Louis mumbles and trails after her. Neither notice the display of a miniature No-Ghost tower once used as a demonstration of the product. Unlike the rest of the museum, it is not surrounded by a protective glass box. A few seconds after they disappear into the museum, the tower activates.

Kalup stops when a small Ouija board appears on the floor in front of the miniature tower. The planchette moves a dozen letters before a dozen ghost guards appear with just as many ghoulish K-9's. The names of the guards are no longer attached to the uniforms, but their place of work is firmly attached to the sleeve, Woard Asylum. The guards center on Kalup and lower their weapons. The hotel tycoon backs away in preparation to run at first then hesitate when they salute him. He studies the unit as they stand at ease, awaiting orders.

"Take out the cat and the dragon. Leave the woman alive," Kalup said in a low tone. The ghostly guards salute once again and disappear. Kalup decides to hang back and wait.

Nako does his happy dance as his friends find him next to a large glass display case. Jesse takes a further step closer as her mouth drops at the sight of the equipment while, Louis manages to shut his own mouth and shakes his head. A bright white light illuminates a laptop that has a nice-sized seventeen-inch screen, which is now darkened.

The keyboard is still attached and has both QWERTY and Aligon characters on the keys. A label on the bottom next to the integrated mouse provides the information of the manufacturer and operating system. It has a Si57 Core 100th generation, which is still used in some applications today. The operating system is Viking 1026, special edition for the anniversary of the manufacturer. A second label indicates that the machine has 200 terabytes for its graphics card along with 1026 terabytes of memory. It is also blu-fi capable which is the oldest of the current network protocols. Louis goes over to study the case as Jesse places one hand upon her head, the other on her hip as she tries to stave off a coming migraine.

"How long has this beast been out of service?" Louis inquires with awe.

"I am proud to say that it has been out of service for a mere ten years," Nako boasts. "It was used in a government cyber unit and has battled many hackers in its day."

"A seasoned warrior," Louis says, with a hint of sarcasm.

"The computer may be seasoned, but we are relying upon Ronan's skills," Jesse reminds her friends.

"This is true, let me get it out so we can get a good look at it," Nako says as he jumps up onto the ledge. He taps the keyboard, but it does not light up. "That's odd."

"Hmm," Louis taps the screen. "I think the backup battery is dead."

"That's unfortunate," Nako frowns.

"I am not going to leave this shop without this computer," Jesse says with a slight growl in her words.

A blue flame springs to life around Jesse and soon change to a brilliant purple color. She makes a few motions with her hands, causing the fire to spin around her body before directing it to the glass cage. The flames roar as they speed through the air and slam into the glass, heating it up rapidly. It starts to glow along the edges as smoke emerges from the seams. Jesse cancels her spell and waits.

As the glass cools down, several edges appear in the middle of each side, creating a cross in the glass on top. Louis touches the glass with the tip of his tail, to test the heat. The entire glass cage falls in quarters, hitting the floor without breaking. Nako taps the closest glass quarters and deduces that the silicon from it is a hybrid of Earth sand mixed with Andromeda sand. Louis reaches in and takes down the computer to look it over with a slight frown.

"This thing is old," Louis said. "Are you sure it just got put out of service ten years ago?"

"Yep. It's at least fifty years old," Nako points out.

"Lets...." Jesse exhales, expressing frustration, "pack it up and get ready to head back to the church. I'm going to see what I can find to make our trip a little easier."

Jesse turns and curses when a ghost guard appears in front of her. She has no time to react as he slams his baton into her, knocking her away and towards a wall. Jesse hits the floor and slides back; the air leaves her lungs from the blow. She fights to regain her breath as Louis goes to her aid.

As soon as the Aligon leaves the seraph cat's side, a ghost dog appears next to Nako and instantly grabs the cat in its mouth. Nako yowls in pain as the dog shakes him violently. Half a dozen guards surround Louis, each with a baton, and start to beat on the dragon. The dog that attacked Nako tosses him into the base of the display. The seraph cat's back folds awkwardly as he hits it.

Jesse lets out an angry sound as she gets to her feet and purple flames explode to life around her body. She sends the fire to the guards around Louis and the dog attacking Nako at the same time. The fire hits the dog first, causing it to yelp in fear and retreat from the fire. The guards notice the fire and yell as they unload guns at the flames. Their sounds are silenced when the flames consume them.

The flame then surrounds Jesse and her friends as she goes to Nako's side. Other guards in the room scream as they unload rifles at the fire. Moments later, they fall and disappear as if reliving the last moments of their lives. Louis speedily examines the seraph cat, immediately deducing that his back is broken as well as suffering deep lacerations into his body. The sound of a planchette sliding across wood catches Jesse's attention.

"Louis," Jesse calls.

"I hear it, keep an eye on Nako," Louis says and stands up.

Jesse comforts the wounded cat as Louis leaps over the flames, landing on the top of another display case. He homes in on the sound of the planchette and heads straight for it. The Ouija board is frantically trying to spell a name as he arrives. Louis lunges at the mini ghost tower, knocking it down. The Ouija board flickers and freezes moments before the Aligon smashes the tower into pieces.

A moan of disappointment echoes from the unsummoned creature as the board disappears. Louis stomps on the main components of the No-Ghost tower, making sure to crush any lenses that produce holograms. He snorts in satisfaction then turns to avoid an attacker. Louis notices that the man is still alive and sneers as he uses his tail to wrap the attacker up in a not-so-gentle squeeze. Kalup is unable to express the pain as the tail tightens around him.

"What are you doing, hairless monkey boy?" Louis demands.

"Louis, come quick, Nako is fading," Jesse calls as she cancels her flame spell.

The Aligon drops his prey and heads back to his friend's side. Jesse strokes Nako's head and speaks to him reassuringly. Nako mews pathetically then tries to catch his breath, his body shuddering with the effort.

"I need to stabilize him," Louis says and reverts back to his human form. He is now shirtless and has a large hole in the back of his pants, exposing his rear end.

"What do you need me to find?" Jesse offers as she stands.

"See if you can find a first aid kit as well as the blood bank. We need type CS," Louis says as he tries to stop the bleeding without hurting the tiny curator further.

"Here," Kalup set several bottles of clear vodka down as well as a roll of toilet paper and bandages. "There is no blood bank in this store."

"Then I will find the vampire's refrigerator," Jesse said. "I will hold my questions for you, Mr. Leyman, until we stabilize my friend."

Jesse leaves on her hurried quest as Louis glares at the hotel tycoon. She heads to the food section and finds the refrigerator fast. It is marked with the symbol universally recognized as 'vampire'. Jesse tries opening it but finds it is locked. She is about to throw a lightning bolt at the door when something more accessible catches her eyes. A piece of paper marked with the symbol of the blood bank hangs from the office door. Underneath it is the words Blood Drive clearly printed with the dates and times of yesterday until midnight.

A flame lights up in Jesse's eyes but she calms it down through a breathing technique. Taking another deep breath in, she opens the door and walks into the office. Several battery-operated refrigerators hum as they keep the precious contents safe. Jesse sorts through the different blood types and finds one donation that matches. Her heart sinks when she notices the name of the donor, Nako Sothpaw. She grabs a few more medical supplies to include IV needles and tubes then exits the office.

"Maybe you had a premonition, my friend," Jesse says grabbing a more things off the shelf as she passes it, and heads back to her friends.

Kalup perks up when Jesse returns with a large number of medical supplies. She ignores him and sets the items down as Nako warbles in pain. Louis swiftly takes stock of the items Jesse brought, to include rubbing alcohol, over the counter pain medication, and a variety of surgical needles. The Aligon sees the blood package then gives Kalup an extremely nasty look. Louis then concentrates on Nako, relying on Jesse's assistance. She keeps Nako's head still as Louis inserts the IV into the cat's neck. The doctor then wraps the neck with a gauze in order to keep it in place.

"Thank you, Jesse, I have it from here," Louis says as he continues to work on his friend.

"How long do you need to stabilize him enough to travel?" Jesse asks.

"Give me a half hour at least," Louis answers.

"I'm going back to looking for the things I was searching for before the attack, anything that will help us return to our destination," Jesse said.

"Find a bag big enough to hold Nako and another for the computer and all of its components," Louis requests.

"Again, why are we leaving a place that is safer than the halls?" Kalup demands.

"This is a Museum of Technology," Jesse informs. "Charlie managed to activate a demonstration unit of the No-Ghost tower. I don't want to know what else is here that he can tap into. I'd rather leave before anything worse comes after us."

"Or even a military bot crashing through these walls," Louis adds.

"These walls are triple reinforced, strong enough to survive a tornado," Kalup says and folds his arms. "Nothing will get through them. I say we will stay."

"You can stay if you want," Jesse reiterates. "My friends and I are leaving."

She once again leaves the hotel tycoon where he stands, ignoring his gaze of surprise. Louis busily works on the seraph cat, giving soft words of comfort to the creature as he uses the supplies brought to him to perform field surgery. Kalup decides to follow the woman.

Jesse peruses the gift shop, finding the bags she needs first and continues to the jewelry section. She pauses, looking around the area and noticing that many of the trinkets are geared towards the now-debunked convention. Items for shamans, witches and divination fill the various display cases and hang from the shelves.

Jesse immediately goes over to the open displays, not bothering to shop the locked cases. She makes a sound of discovery when she finds the items she is looking for among the trinkets. A necklace with the centerpiece of a crescent moon, a bracelet with a deer surrounded by trees carved into real wood, and a silver broach meticulously molded into a bow drawn back with arrow in the center.

Jesse nods as she places the three items in a smaller drawstring bag and ties it on the belt loop of her jeans as she walks.

She pauses by the statue of Bastet and looks up at it. The statue is still glowing and flashing as invisible ghouls tap on the glass doors. Jesse nods as she studies the statue, walking around it to take in every detail. She smiles at the golden band around the middle of the tail. It has a Museum of Past Modern History stamp with Nako's signature carved in the gold. Jesse stands in front of the statue, her mood still uplifted as she figures that it is carved so well that it could stand up and walk out of the gift shop if it had the will to do so.

"You know you are stealing, right?" Kalup asks as he approaches from the darkness.

"We are in crisis, Kalup," Jesse answers calmly as she faces him. "In such circumstances, the laws allow for survivors to do whatever necessary to survive the situation they are in."

"I think you should let the seraph cat die," Kalup abruptly changes the subject.

"Excuse me?" Jesse arches an eyebrow as she folds her arms.

"The cat is a bad influence on you, the Aligon even more so," Kalup continues as he purposely invades her personal space. "I don't want you to see either one anymore."

"Have you lost your mind?" Jesse asks.

"You are mine," Kalup says with a definite tone as he leans in to kiss her. He ends up frozen in place then lifted by a strong force as he floats away from Jesse.

"No, I am not," Jesse retorts.

She does a simple motion with her finger and Kalup yells as he goes flying into the gift shop. He lands with a crash somewhere in the food section of the shop. Jesse releases her spell on the tycoon when he is no longer in sight. She exhales and once again looks at the statue. Her attention goes to the glass door when she hears something big beating against it. A frown comes to her features when she notices that it too is currently invisible.

"I need an ankh and a very sharp carving knife," Jesse says aloud. She turns away to return to the part of the shop where she had picked up her trinkets.

Twenty minutes of foraging later, Jesse returns to her friends and places the duffle bag she found for the seraph cat next to the injured cat. Louis nods his approval as he checks Nako's pulse. Jesse goes over to the computer with her other bag and puts it, accessories, and all, inside. She zips it up and pulls the pack onto her back, making sure the straps are comfortable for her arms. A low rumble alerts them both that a military bot is close.

"Did you find anything good?" Louis asks as Jesse bends down to check on Nako.

"I found a few trinkets that will help," Jesse answers. "We are also taking Bastet with us."

"Okay," Louis says then whips his head in her direction. "What? How?"

"Tarot Pneuma is not the only thing I can do, Louis," Jesse reminds him.

"Alright, help me with Nako," Louis says.

Jesse holds the duffle bag open as Louis places his patient inside. The wings are held down gently as the bag is zipped up. Louis studies the fit and nods, the duffle bag holds the cat still and allows his head to peek out. Nako grumble sleepily about the medication Louis gave him for pain. The Aligon then returns to his dragon form as he stands up and picks up the duffle bag, with a great deal of care, by the handles. When Nako does not shift, he relaxes his shoulders.

"What happened to Kalup? I thought I heard him scream," Louis asks.

"You did, I tossed him somewhere into the gift shop," Jesse answers. "Let's get back before Aegis gets impatient."

"And that robot gets through the wall," Louis says.

The rumbling of the bot catches Jesse's attention, causing her to scowl. She turns and leads the way back through the gift shop to the statue of Bastet. Louis helps Jesse scramble up onto the base that the giant cat sits on. She thanks him, then jumps along with the Aligon when they hear the bot slam into the rear wall of the shop somewhere in the museum section.

Jesse takes out the knife she had found as well as the ankh necklace. She puts the jewelry on before scratching symbols into the chest of the statue. She speaks her incantation in a hushed voice as she pricks one of her fingers and traces the blood onto the words she had just carved. Jesse continues her chant as she turns her back to the statue and crouches down, sitting as if she too is the statue. Several seconds pass and the military bot once again slams into the wall.

"Jesse, I don't mean to hurry you," Louis calls.

The Aligon jumps when the statue and Jesse both twist their heads. The golem then turns to face Louis with purple glowing eyes. Jesse's body starts to glow softly as she levitates up and onto the back of the statue. Bastet then stands and stretches in feline fashion then once again look at Louis.

"Whoa," Louis takes a step back.

"It takes a minute for the connection to occur," Jesse says, her voice coming from the statue.

"Wouldn't it be easier to use the Dragon Tarot on me instead?" Louis asks, scolding the young woman.

"Yes, but you don't come with a built-in ghost shield and the unfamiliar deck is also unreliable at this time," Jesse answers.

"You do make a point," Louis acknowledges, then scrambles up the leg of the statue to the back. "After this, make sure you rest."

"I will rest after we get the hell out of this building," Jesse retorts. "Please make sure that I don't fall off."

"Don't worry, you are not going anywhere," Louis assures her. "I've got you."

"I'm cold," Nako mews.

"Hold on, friend, we are going to go quickly," Jesse says.

Jesse swings the left front paw of the statue at the glass doors, shattering them. The sharp wind clears the glass from the threshold as the golem stalks from the base and into the hall. The gold symbols upon the head and neck intensify as the cat-snakes reappear. Instead of attacking, however, they cower at the statue and retreat down the hall.

Jesse presses the statue forward, following the fleeing ghouls, reaching the full size No-Ghost tower in no time. She makes an angry sound as she destroys the item as they run past it, shattering the lantern, and putting an end to the Ouija board summoning. Louis ducks low, close to Jesse's body to keep her aboard. He frowns when he notices the amount of heat coming from her skin.

They speed down the hall and round a few corners, heading straight for the vendor hall. Jesse pushes the statue to a top speed, pressing through hordes of spirits along the way. The built-in shields continue to perform by keeping the specters at bay.

A swear comes from the statue as Jesse slides it to a stop then jumps back as a large talon swing at them from the darkness. Louis sits up to see what has stopped progress. His jaw drops open as a beast with the eyes of a cat, wings and body of a dragon, talons of a bird, and head of an unknown beast melt into the half-light of the hall. Flames lick at its lips and appear to giggle as they dance.

"What the hell is that?" Louis asks.

"I don't know, I've never seen this spirit before," Jesse scowls. The statue's eyes widen in recognition. "Wait, the stained-glass."

The beast bellows as it spits flames at Jesse and her companions. Mad laughter echoes in the halls along with the roar of the flames. Jesse reacts by moving to the left, destroying a wall to avoid the elemental weapon. The attacking beast howls in rage as the flames miss their mark. Jesse breaks through another wall behind the beast and pours on the speed to get away. Undeterred, the attacker pursues its prey.

The golem enters the vendor space and heads toward the hall to get to the church with the fire demon hot on her heels. Jesse does not have time to give any warning as she jumps as high as she can get the statue to move. At the same time, the military bot blocking the hall fires the cannon. The creature behind Jesse does not react as fast and is struck by the ammunition, shrieking more in anger than in pain. Jesse lands and cuts to the right, going down a different passageway to get to her destination. The military bot goes into pursuit mode but does not get far as the fire demon tears it apart in anger.

The sound of hard stone against concrete echoes in the passage as Jesse continues to push the limits of the statue as well as her own abilities. The temperature of Jesse's body increases a little more, concerning Louis tremendously. The hall starts to incline somewhat as a dead-end loom in front of the fleeing trio. Jesse growls as she decides to go through the wall in order to reach her destination.

Louis holds tight as the statue destroys the wall and leaps into the air beyond. The Aligon swears, loudly, when he notes that the church is at least three stories below their location. The statue starts to fall apart as Jesse loses consciousness. Louis calls her name but does not get a response.

The free-fall is short-lived as someone grabs Louis's tail, causing him to grunt in pain. He makes sure he has a firm grip on Nako before he looks back. Aegis is holding the dragon's tail with one hand; the other arm is cradling Jesse. The Guardian's wings easily keep the entire group aloft.

"She has a fever, what happened?" Aegis inquires.

"A whole lot, actually," Louis responds. "Can we get inside the church? I want to check Nako's wounds and make sure that Jesse is not burning."

Aegis studies Jesse for a moment then descends to the floor. Louis exhales in relief when his feet touch the ground, taking pressure off of his tail. The Aligon twists his appendage to make sure he is still in working order. The Guardian lands next, making sure not to awaken Jesse. He folds his wings in a way that assures the woman is not disturbed. Jesse twitches but remains asleep. Aegis' features turn to concern as he studies the woman. Low rumbling from down the hall alerts Louis as the cavern begins to shake.

"That is not thunder," Louis says to the Guardian. "It sounds like a large group of military bots have followed us."

"We are under attack," Aegis frowns as several bots exit the tunnels. "Take Jesse and get inside the church."

"Be careful, they are not made from materials from Earth," Louis says as he takes hold of the woman with his tail.

"That is good to know," Aegis replies.

Louis hastily enters the church with his friends as seven military bots spread out, flanking each other. The camera above the tunnel zooms in as Aegis pulls his sword and charges with lightning speed towards the military bots. He swings his blade to cleave one mechanical monstrosity in half. The blade whistles through the hair and slides against the armor of the bot, creating sparks and a simple scratch for his troubles. Aegis stops a short distance from the attackers and looks at his sword in surprise that it did not work.

The air moves above him, catching his attention. When he looks up, he curses then disappears as the giant circular saws of the bot he attacked swing to cleave him in half. Instead, the bot's saw blade strikes one of its companions, slicing it in half. Aegis reappears in the air, taking in the damage. His wings take him higher to make sure that he is out of range of the bot's weapons. Aegis concentrates on the blades of the defeated bot and detaches them.

The giant circular saws float up at his command, levitating next to him. The last six bots center their cannons on the flying being then find out they are out of ammunition. The bots then bring up the machine guns as Aegis commands the floating blades to spin rapidly. The air sings as the blades spin at least twice their usual speed. The bots fire upon the Guardian. He blocks the bullets using one of the two saw blades. He sends the other one toward his attackers. The blade goes from vertical to horizontal as it spins a mere six feet from the floor, speeding to the formation.

It slices through the first four bots then gets stuck inside of the fifth one, disabling them. The last bot sends up an antenna to request backup. Aegis uses the second blade to slice through the bot and antenna vertically then brings it back to slice through the rest of the bot horizontally. The blade then sails until it slams into the wall above the tunnel, destroying the camera. Aegis once again lands upon the ground and listens, concentrating on the tunnels. He hears nothing in the immediate area except the heartbeats of the frightened mortals inside the church. Aegis snaps his wings, sending out a cold wind before he folds them down once again. He turns and walks back into the church, confidently.

In another room of the hotel, the holotube replays the skirmish between Aegis and the military bots. A ghostly sound of frustration fills the void as the observer sees the camera destroyed in the end. The door behind whooshes open then closes, allowing the guest to enter easily. Charlie turns and lets out a moan of fright as the flame beast stalks into the room. It gurgles as it changes form.

The ghost relaxes as the woman saunters over to him and places a hand on his shoulder. He turns as she pushes a few buttons to change the view of a camera in another location. Charlie sees a group of prestigious buildings neatly sitting upon a field of green. The words 'Monroe College of Metamorphism' are displayed proudly on the side of the largest building.

"Destroy it," the woman commands. Charlie cackles as he fiddles with the controls. The camera starts to shake as it moves towards the structure.

CHAPTER SEVEN

Jesse's Dream

The wind whistles through the brokage of seven oak trees, imitating the hymns that once traveled with the breeze. Jesse lets out a whoop of joy as she travels through the trees, dipping and spiraling in acrobatic fashion towards the edge of the grove. She breaks through the brush and centers on the small grey church sitting among rolling hills. She circles the building, taking in the details of several stained-glass windows that depict various legends of a great book. All but two of the windows are faded at this time. Jesse recognizes the window of the woman kneeling in a field of flowers on the side of the building. She circles to the back and sees the second window of Aegis battling a beast.

Jesse identifies the beast as the one that attacked her in the hall with the strange flames giggling from its mouth. She hovers in front of the window as she studies the scene. The Guardian is dressed in leather-like armor and is lifting a mighty golden sword above his head, aiming it towards the crown of the beastly demon. The creature, in turn, has a ratty tail wrapped around the neck of the angel in an attempt to kill him before the sword strikes. The currents lift Jesse up, sending her to the top of the high steeple. She lands and take a deep breath in.

"I think I am dreaming," Jesse chirps and pauses. "Did that come from me? Am I a bird? I have wings? I don't have time for this nonsense, I have to get Nako out of the hotel."

"Be patient," a woman mildly scolds.

"Who is that?" Jesse inquires.

Shadows fall over the glass when a large swarm of ravens rushes in on the wind. They caw and harass Jesse as they make their way to a large building standing just over the hill from the church. Jesse curses at them, then swears again as the winds lift her up and send her after the ravens. She corrects her position and uses her wings to press forward at a surprisingly great speed. She is soon flying just above the flock as they approach the perimeter.

Dogs bark and jump at the flying birds in an attempt to capture them in midflight. Jesse follows the ravens as they move past the giant chain link fence, wary about landing on it. She banks past the guard towers and continues toward a large late century Victorian mansion. Jesse recognizes it from the picture and frowns as the winds push her onward.

"The asylum, why am I here?" Jesse muses.

The ravens' caws mingle with the screams and laughter of those residing in the building. Jesse follows the ravens as they fly past the barred windows and spiral towards the top of the hall tower. They crest it with the ravens landing on the large concrete sign hanging just above the entrance door. Jesse flies past the cackling birds and briefly catches a glimpse of the words on the concrete. They read: Welcome to Woard Asylum, home for notoriously insane criminals. Jesse banks and circles back to an old dead tree, landing on a solid limb.

"Okay. I need to figure out the puzzle before I can wake up," Jesse says to herself.

As Jesse muses her current situation, an old air conditioning unit huffs and labors near the back of the building. Jesse turns and watches the item, curiously. She flies over to another, closer, limb as green smoke rises from the interior of the machine as it coughs and finally collapses. Dried grass and leaves around the unit start to smolder immediately then catch fire. A woman fades into sight as the flames begin to die down, having consumed the tinder around it. Jesse tilts her head as she studies the familiar woman. Her eyes blink and she lets out a high pitch tweet when she recognizes her.

"Wait, that's Irava!" Jesse exclaims.

The woman, Irava, is younger and healthier than Jesse remembers from the meeting. Her eyes now hold a strangely yellow-orange flame within as a mischievous smirk grace her features. Irava bends and holds her hand just above the dying embers. She speaks a few words and starts to cackle. Jesse jumps when the flames crackle back to life, their sound reflecting the laughter of the woman. Jesse takes to wing as the flames run up the tree she is perched upon and reduces it to ashes. She then flies into an open window to escape the ravenous fire. Irava calls to the fire and wraps it around her own body. Her body changes, taking on the element eagerly. Lunatic laughter escapes the flames as she leaps into an open window.

Jesse flies through the hall, landing on a light fixture to catch her breath. Her head turns when she hears the laughter and then sees the flames catch in the office she had just left. The fire spreads rapidly, forcing Jesse back into the air to avoid it. Staff and prisoners alike scream in pain or, surprisingly, pleasure as the fire consumes them. Jesse finds herself flying behind a dozen staff members towards the entrance. She pulls up and doubles back, avoiding the fire when she notices the doors do not open. The fire makes quick work of those who try to open the doors, consuming them. Instead of dying, they start laughing and dancing in the fire.

Electricity shuts off and the doors to the prisoners' cells open automatically. Many of the prisoners assassinate the first person they see right before the fire kills them. Jesse avoids more flames and ducks into the first open cell she can find. She screams when she almost collides with Charlie. His straitjacket is untied as the head nurse provides oral pleasure to him. He laughs as he tries to swat the bird down.

Flames enter his cell, stunning him momentarily before he starts to once again laugh. The nurse turns around and stands up from her precarious position when she notices them. The flames pause and reshape into the form of a nude woman. Jesse decides to duck through the open window, through the bars, as the fire mistress seduces and consumes both Charlie and the nurse. Charlie hollers in pain and pleasure as he dies.

Jesse spirals skyward as the flames gut the entire building, reducing much of it and the victims inside to nothing more than a pile of ash. Jesse hovers in the air as she takes in what she had just witnessed. Even though this is a dream, the heat of the flames is entirely too real for her. She curses under her breath when she sees Irava saunter from the flames, still engulfed within them. She smiles as she turns her sights toward the four guard towers a mile from the main building.

"Now what..." Jesse starts then immediately dodges as the flames try to grab her once again. "Nope, out of here."

Jesse turns and flies with all of her might toward the guard towers. At the same time Irava cackles as she points to one of the structures, giving the flames a strong command. The fire springs from her body and rushes past her from the building itself, speeding to the destination. Jesse reaches the tower first and lands upon it to catch her breath. She hears the dogs barking and turns to see the flames heading straight towards them. The fire twists and contorts until they form a strange beast running, it's eyes firmly focused upon the towers. It is similar to the beast on the stained-glass.

Dogs bark and rush forward to attack the apparition, jumping when they reach it to get at the throat. The flames grab each animal and rapidly consume it, scarcely allowing a yelp escape. Before Jesse can react, flames surround the tower, limiting escape for those who are flightless. Several guards jump through a window in order to escape. It proves futile as they are incinerated upon reaching the ground. The flames barge up the tower stairs and into the top room. More men shout as they unload their weapons at the flame beast. It laughs as it lunges forward, devouring the guards in an instant. The fire bursts through the roof and Jesse once again takes to wing. She looks around then remembers the church.

"Right, going to church once again," Jesse says to herself as she heads in the direction of the small grey building.

Thunderclaps from the heavens and the winds pick up considerably, fighting Jesse as she flies into it. Irava jumps from the sound then scowls as she witnesses the gathering clouds. She focuses her attention on the grey church in the distance. She sneers at the structure and points to it with a harsh command to the flames.

Jesse hears the words and looks back briefly to see the fire gather up and launch towards the same building she is striving to reach. A ferocious sound emerges from it as it increases its speed. Jesse presses forward, increasing her speed when the flames get close enough to take out her tail feathers. She crests the fence and glides low along the ground to get avoid the head winds.

The fire takes down the same obstacle with unnerving ease as it continues toward the church. A strong, cold, wind flies past Jesse and slams into the flames, causing them to shriek in anger and die back. Jesse takes the opportunity to increase the distance between herself and the flames. She pulls up at the door and lands on the stairs, pushing on it with her tiny body to see if she could get in. The doors do not budge. Jesse swears and turns to face the flames. Her defiance turns to surprise as a second figure appears between the fire and the humble holy site. Irava frowns when she sees the Guardian and takes her time as she backs into the smoke and flames of the building to avoid detection.

"Aegis!" Jesse cheers. "Oh damn, I don't think he can hear me."

Rain starts to fall, lightly at first. The flames react to the mist with a moan of rage as it continues to press forward. Lightning flashes in Aegis' steel-blue eyes as he concentrates upon the fire. The sound of thunder echoes when the fires rear up, once again morphing into the beast of flames.

The Guardian pulls his blade as his large wings spread out in preparation for his charge. He jumps back and into the sky when the flames snap at him. The fire attack again and misses its mark as Aegis moves to the side with unnerving speed, then takes off the head of the beast. It withers back then renews itself, attacking once more with a new head. Aegis moves up and uses his wings to increase the winds, blowing the flame beast down to the ground. It crouches down and roars in defiance. Aegis looks over his shoulder at the heavens and calls out to it.

Jesse looks up and chirps in surprise as the rain becomes a torrent of water and soaks her feathers. She backs up and keeps herself as close to the door as possible. A large string of tweets escapes her as she shakes herself dry then once again focus on the battle. Lightning streaks across the sky and thunder echoes all around as rain washes through the now burnt-out hull of the asylum, extinguishing whatever flame is left in the structure. The fire beast roars in agony as it withers in pain. Aegis watches the beast for a moment then lifts his sword and dives towards the it. His blade penetrates the hide at first, causing a squeal of pain to exit the monster's form.

The Guardian then pulls the sword and swings at the head of his opponent to decapitate it. A string of angry words come from both Aegis and Jesse when the sword goes through the air. The beast moves as quick as it can back to the asylum, water hissing against it as the flames die out. Before it can reach shelter, the flame beast collapses, turning into a pile of smoldering leaves then disintegrating into ashes. The rain tapers off as Aegis approaches the spot where the creature had collapsed. He steps on it and kicks the ashes to make sure the fire goes all the way out.

Jesse exhales in relief when the fire does not rekindle and leans back against the doors. She cries out in surprise when she falls through the wooden barriers and lands on the floor of the church as a human. Jesse grumbles as she sits up, holding her head. Her actions freeze when she sees a lace sleeve hugging her arm. Her eyes travel from the sleeve to the rest of her body, noting that her whole outfit has changed to a white gown made of lace and silk.

A state of shock takes over her as she gets to her feet. Pain racks through her stemming from her left ankle and she falls back towards the floor. An arm around her waist holds her up and steadies her as she regains her footing. Jesse glances around the church in awe at the scene. Although there are no people present, the inner sanctuary appears much livelier than she recalls. The wood is warmer, gold encircles all of the stained-glass windows, and silver is inlaid upon the carvings and words all around the room.

Jesse turns her attention to the largest window on the back wall and notices a considerable change. Instead of Aegis in battle, he is standing at peace with a likeness of her at his side. To the right of the main image is a depiction of Louis in his golden dragon form with Nako sitting next to him. To the left of the main depiction has an image of Artemis leaning against a tree, watching the couple in the center.

"Okay, at least I'm not a bird anymore," Jesse says to herself. "Now, where is Aegis?"

"He is not here. He is still in the realm of the awakened," the same woman's voice that spoke to her before answers. "I'm sure he's protecting you while you are asleep."

"Keep calm, Jesse," Jesse cautions herself as she turns to the person holding her up. She takes a deep breath in when she sees the familiar woman. "You are the lady in the stained-glass window."

"I am," the woman agrees with a warm smile. "My name is Jessica."

"Whoa…." Jesse moves away from the woman and stares at her.

"I know, very unsettling, isn't it?" Jessica chuckles at her guest's features.

"You are aware of just the half of it," Jesse answers.

Jessica flashes a bright smiles and lifts both arms up as if showing off. Her white linen tunic reaches all the way down to her sandal-covered feet. Her complexion is slightly darker than Jesse's, and she is also a little heavier. Jesse guesses that the woman may be a year or two older than her.

Jessica turns around at a slow speed as if to profile, her braided hair shifting with her movements. The guest shakes herself out of her stupor and once again takes in her surroundings. The windows no longer hold biblical scenes, but each has a peaceful picture of flowers or nature within. Jesse glances at the doors and sees they are still closed tight

"You did make it to the church," Jessica said, catching her guest's attention once more. "You passed out and are now dreaming."

"I figured that when I was the bird," Jesse agrees. "You were the voice that told me to have patience?"

'I was," Jessica nods. "I wanted you to see what you are up against when you wake up."

"Okay," Jesse rubs her temples as she sits down on a pew. "Why did you bring me here? I need to get my seraph cat friend to the hospital as soon as I can."

"Nako will be alright. Louis is an accomplished doctor," Jessica assures. "He is also worried about you. Apparently, he feels you are a very good friend."

"Wait, how do you know my name, let alone those of my friends?" Jesse stares at the woman.

"I've got a couple of things going for me," Jessica smiles and sit across from her guest on a chair. "I was a clairvoyant in life as well as a Spell Caster, to use the term that Aegis developed for anyone that has metaphysical manifestation abilities. I'm also responsible for half of the strong force keeping the ghosts from entering the church for now. But our powers are fading, and we are exhausted."

"We?" Jesse arches an eyebrow and takes a fast look around. "We who?"

Sadness reflects upon Jessica as she lifts her tunic and takes a step back. The visitor takes a sharp breath of surprise when she sees the little girl with tiny angel wings lying curled up on the floor. The child uncurls and rolls onto her back to stretch in the light of the inner sanctum. A cascade of black curly hair frames her angelic face. She blinks sleep from her steel-blue eyes and sits up to focus on Jesse. A gasp escapes from the girl before she jumps to her feet and hurries over to Jessica, asking to be picked up. The request is obliged with a small scolding from the mother of the child.

Jesse rubs her eyes then pulls her hands down her face as she tries to run through her mind what it is she is seeing. She takes a deep breath then removes her hands to put her attention back on her hostess. Jesse meets the girl's eyes as the child lays her head upon her mother's shoulder.

"That's Aegis' daughter," Jesse points out.

"She is," Jessica agrees. "Her name is Anna. I was carrying her when the Flames of Madness surrounded me."

"Flames of Madness," Jesse stands up. "Wait, Irava. The asylum."

"Calm down, easy now," Jessica says gently.

"Okay, Okay, Okay," Jesse runs her fingers through her hair. She takes a deep breath. "Tell me what happened."

"I think it is easier on me and Anna if I showed you," Jessica offers.

Jessica looks behind her at the large window, prompting her visitor to do the same. The glass wiggles and erupts in red flame as a scene from the past comes into vivid life. Jessica blocks a stream of fire and casts a spell to push it back. Maddened laughter echoes from the fire as it bounces around.

Jessica places an arm on her stomach and falls to her knees, panting. The flames make a gleeful sound as the fire roars toward her. She sees it and raises an arcane shield then holds tight as the flames squeeze onto it. Jessica strains against the weight for a second then lets out a mighty yell as she pushes out on her shield and disburses the flames once more.

The shield is no more as her hands fall to the ground. Her head lowers as she seeks to catch her breath. Jessica looks up just in time for the flames to crash into her. They lift her up and slam her against an aging wall, pushing fiercely onto her. Jessica wails in pain and it is answered with a bellow of anger. Her screams soon turn to maddened laughter as the flames start to consume her. Aegis lands and is immediately attacked by Jessica.

"Ah, so now the mortal is infected," Irava boasts in the background. "What are you going to do now, Guardian? If the flames consume her completely, she becomes a part of my madness."

Storm clouds gather overhead as Jessica continues to attack and burn. A deluge of rain dumps from the sky, slamming into the fire. Jessica screams in pain along with the Flames of Madness. A bolt of lightning erupts from the sky and strikes the suffering woman, sending her backwards and now through the wall.

Aegis lets out a sound of shock as he hurries over toward Jessica. He lifts her up into his arms as a small sound escapes him. Jessica meets his gaze with her own, her eyes are clear from the madness. Her hand trembles as she lifts it and strokes Aegis' cheek once. Her eyes close as her life force leaves her, and her hand falls back down to her side. Aegis gently shakes the woman as if asking her to wake up. Instead, Jessica takes her very last breath. The window once again returns to the scene Jesse saw when she first arrived as Aegis's anguish-filled cry echoes in the halls.

"Oh, wow," Jesse whispers. She looks down to see Anna now sitting in her lap. "How did you get here?"

"She became brave while you were watching my memories," Jessica said with a smile.

"Alright, I'm trying to put it all together now," Jesse said. "I've not seen the flames, but I did see that beast in the halls of the hotel. I remember Irava in the meeting. She is the Mistress of the Flames."

"The Flames of Madness are generated by the burning of souls. The more tormented, talented, or insane the soul, the stronger the flame and the more powerful the Mistress that it feeds." Jessica warns.

"It is not by fate or chance that she chose the 300th anniversary of the Mystical Paranormal Convention to add to her collection," Jesse holds her head. "The entire hotel is filled with practitioners of all type and a lot of them died."

"Everything that was built upon this ground before and after the asylum has fallen to the Flames of Madness," Jessica adds.

"Asylum, human meat factory, illegal orphanage," Jesse recalls the list sent to her by the PIU officers. "Oh my."

"Also, the Mistress does not always consume her victims," Jessica informs. "She also seduces them as well. Those she keeps alive, becomes her servants. To disobey her is instant death."

"Irava mentioned a seductress that Kalup summoned with the Ouija software," Jesse muses. "I wonder if...."

"The seductress was her, I'd say a good possibility," Jessica finishes. "She can use him to pull in more retainers."

"Kalup has been adamantly after me," Jesse admits.

"Not good. It means that Irava, as you call her, is trying to recruit or destroy you for some reason, Jesse," Jessica frowns as the windows start to darken. "Tell Aegis that I love him, and we forgave him a long time ago."

The building shakes violently. Jessica reels back as if she is struck by an opponent. Anna runs over to her mother in order to be comforted. Jesse stands up and looks about, noting that the windows have taken on a red glow, as if fire is surrounding the church. Jessica regains her footing and looks around as she picks up Anna. She turns to the back window and mutters a few words under her breath. The entire scene has taken on a dark, foreboding, look. She turns to her guest.

"It's time for you to wake up," Jessica says. "The flames that attacked us have somehow returned. Go through the front door, hurry, that's the way back to awareness."

"Thank you, Jessica," Jesse says and goes to the door. "Wait, does Aegis know about the child?"

"Will you tell him?" Jessica requests.

The flames break through the glass and rush in, surrounding Jessica and Anna. It tries to attack the two victims. Jessica holds her daughter tight as the fire hit a strong shield and yowls to show it's displeasure about the barrier. Jesse fights down her instinct to assist, knowing that the flames will eventually win as they did when Jessica was alive. The guest pushes open the door to escape the church. She hesitates when a great void yawns in front of her.

Words do not have time to form from her as the doors fall out of her hands. Jesse looks around and swears as the entire church starts to fall apart around her. The floor disappears and Jesse cries out in fear as she falls into a void. Her cries of fear are soon silenced as she finds herself falling through blue skies and clouds. She looks at her arms and notes that she is not a bird this time.

"Where, what, who?" Jesse looks around. "Jessica?"

There is no answer as Jesse continues to drop through the atmosphere. Her descent slows down and she witnesses the last of a battle between Aegis and a more powerful Guardian Angel. Aegis wins the battle then turns and leaves the room. Jesse gasps when her tumble speeds up again from there. Several memories from her history fly past her as she continues to descend. The most recent memory of her grandmother breaks her heart. Jesse closes her eyes to rein in her emotions. When she opens them, she finds herself standing on solid ground outside of her school.

"I'm telling you, Bartholomew, that the code you gave us is not working," a deep-voiced man says with obvious annoyance in is words.

"Are you sure it's one of our machines? That code works on all of them," the man, Bartholomew, retorts.

"It has your name on it," the first man said.

Jesse faces the man that is talking on a phone and recognizes him as the Knight of GUMA that Nako had spoken to in the restaurant. Several disturbing crashes and explosions catch Jesse's attention, and she turns in the direction of her college. She lets out a cry of surprise and anger when she sees a five-story construction bot tearing through her college buildings as if they are nothing more than paper. It's multiple arms and tank treads are trampling the entire building system. It is ripping through every wall, roofline, and even the floors. It has already made its way through over half of the campus and is now aiming towards the dorms.

"No, this should not be happening," Jesse shouts to the winds.

Lightning strikes the bot, originating from a clear blue sky. It stops for a moment as the lights that make up the eyes go out. The bot reroutes the burnt circuit and lights back up to continue ahead. Slow mechanized laughter emerges from the speaker as it presses forward. The sound of a gong echoes in the air as two men beat upon it trying desperately to break the outer skin of the bot, to no avail. A woman runs into the dorm and pulls the fire alarm. It warbles as the students exit their rooms and ultimately the building. When they see the giant bot, they quickly return to assist their friends.

"Damn it, Donner, destroy the thing!" the man next to Jesse shouts to the two attacking the robot.

"We're trying, but the damn thing won't break!" Donner shouts back.

"Okay Octavius, I sent over another code," Bartholomew says from the phone.

"Still not stopping," Octavius replies. "Where is the battery for this thing?"

Jesse screams, causing the man to pause as if he had heard her. The dorm building falls with one blow from the construction bot. It laughs, uncontrollably, then turns its attention to Jesse's family home. Jesse tries to rush forward but finds that she is stuck in place. She looks down to see her feet have somehow become stuck in the mud.

"Aunt Aggie!" Jesse calls out.

"Donner, go to the house and make sure no one alive is in there," Octavius shouts to his son. "Bartholomew, you and your partner are in deep trouble. The Monroe College is a recent addition to the Museum."

"I didn't order the bot to destroy anything, I don't even know how it got there," Bartholomew defends himself. "I'll have to contact Kalup Leyman to see if he has something to do with it."

Jesse watches in horror as the construction bot rips into her family home. To her it is like watching the destruction in slow motion. Tears start to well up inside her as she falls to her knees. Glass shatters as Donner jumps out the window furthest from the bot cradling something next to his chest. He swears audibly yet keeps his arm tight to assure the small being stays with him during their quick retreat.

Donner grunts as he uses his long legs to puts distance between himself and the construction bot. No sooner does he clear the space that the last wall falls to the ground. The bot laughs uncontrollably as it sets its sights on the megachurch across the street. It makes a gleeful sound as it rumbles toward the structure.

Jesse does not even turn when she hears the construction bot start its destruction of the megachurch. Octavius and his family curse as they hurry across the street. Jesse hears screams from those caught in the building as the robot does its work. The sounds soon start to fade as does the mechanical laughter as darkness envelopes Jesse. Its overwhelming presence silents everything around her. She is kept company by her own panicked breathing. She tries to calm it, but her pulse quickens instead.

"Come on Jesse, wake up," Jesse says to herself, then whimpers. "Please, just wake up."

CHAPTER EIGHT

The Departure

The church is buzzing with various hushed conversations as Louis exits the small room at the rear of the stage. The Aligon uses his tail to close the door as he shifts the backpack upon his shoulder. He takes a deep breath in and out as he rolls his neck in preparation for an uphill battle with Ronan. The programmer sees the Aligon approaching him and decides to try and ignore him. Louis sits down next to the human, undeterred by the reaction he gets.

"Okay Ronan. We have the computer," Louis says, bringing out the item. "It has a kinetic charger, so I made sure it was fully powered before I brought it to you."

"What is this? Are you insulting me?" Ronan looks at the antiquated laptop. "You expect me to crack into my software using this doorstop?"

"It has been used to fight cyber criminals before it was retired. In fact, it has more features on it than modern machines, to include your own," Louis points out.

"No," Ronan said flatly.

"What?" Louis sneers.

"I changed my mind; I don't want to assist. You are going to have to find another way," Ronan says and turns his back on the Aligon.

"*I know you did not just say that to me, human waste bag,*" Louis snarls, switching to his native tongue.

"*These worthless people are unworthy of me sacrificing my life,*" Ronan retaliates. "*You want to save them, go ahead but I will not be a part of this. Good luck, dragon turd.*"

"*Oh, ho, ho, you are funny,*" Louis says.

A ruckus near the entrance captures Louis's attention. Ronan tries to take advantage of the Aligon's distraction and tips away. He gets two steps from his tormentor then swears as the tail of the Aligon wraps around his ankle Louis glances back at the programmer then reasserts his attention on the door itself.

Kalup, wrapped in bandages, walks into the small structure to the amazement of everybody. He takes a few more steps in then sets the large, heavy, bag he has been carrying on the floor. He turns it over and dumps out a large amount of food and drinks. The people all gasp and shout praises as they rush forward to grab as much of the bounty as they can.

"No, I don't think I want anything," Christine refuses a snack from a fellow survivor. "Kalup, how the hell did you get through this place unharmed?"

"Do I look unharmed?" Kalup asks, showing off his bandages. "I followed Jesse and her friends to the gift shop, but they abandoned me on advice from the Aligon."

"Excuse me, what?" Louis asks and raises an eyebrow. "I said no such thing. You wanted to stay at the gift shop, so we adhered to your wishes."

"Your words mean nothing, space devil," the wild-haired leader of The Faithful declares. "It is apparent that Kalup Leyman is our true savior, not your evil witch. He will lead us safely to the outside!"

A large group of people shout out praises and celebrate lavishly upon hearing the words. Louis glances around at the happy people as if they themselves have become insane. He also notices that a handful of people are sitting quietly on one side of the church. They appear nervous around the large amount of The Faithful that occupy the space. Ronan tries to free himself from the Aligon and succeeds for the moment. The programmer decides to mingle among the crowd of those celebrating to get away from his antagonist. Kalup waits a moment before holding up his hand. The place goes silent once more.

"I need to see Jesse first," Kalup said. "Where is she?"

"Out of your reach, hairless monkey boy," Louis answers.

"She is in the back room turning the LORD's Angel into a devil with her wicked sins," The Faithful leader informs Kalup.

"Really? I'm going to have to interrupt that," Kalup said. "If the dragon moves, kill him."

Louis frowns at the order and the way that The Faithful have transfixed on him. He folds his arms as Kalup walks, confidently, to the rear of the stage. Several men start towards the Aligon.

Louis spread his arms and crouches as he lets out a charismatic dragon roar, the sound echoing deep into the caverns of the hotel. The men hesitate and decide not to continue or pursue the orders given by Kalup. Louis's tail waves behind him, a clear indicator of his agitation, as he once again folds his arms. The Aligon decides to let Kalup come face to face with the Guardian.

The door to the church office opens and closes softly as Kalup lets himself in. He looks around and notices that it seems more of a crypt than an office. Nako is resting on a padded chair; his breathing has become closer to normal as he sleeps. Jesse lays upon her back on a large rectangular concrete box. Her arms are to her side and her jacket is unzipped now. The rise and fall of her bosom indicate that she is still alive and sleeping.

Kalup looks around the room to take in the small multiuse space. He notices the life-like statue of a winged man standing in the corner, not too far from Jesse. Kalup decides to ignore the statue and make short work of the cat after he has his way with the now-defenseless woman. An evil smile graces his features as he moves towards her. He leans over, placing his hands on either side of her head, and draws close to kiss her on her luscious lips. In the next instant, Kalup is struggling to breathe, let alone swallows as a large hand now holds him by his neck against a wall and away from his quarry. The hotel tycoon blinks in surprise when he meets the angry steel gaze of what he thought was a statue.

"I am surprised at your audacity, mortal, for coming into this room when I specifically told all but one to stay out," Aegis informs. "To further infuriate me, you try to solicit favors from an unconscious woman."

"I have been told that she will be mine," Kalup manages.

"Really?" Aegis draws the man uncomfortably close. "By whom?"

Jesse cries out all of the sudden. Her sounds catch the attention of both men and awakening Nako. She balls her hands into fists and punches the stone as she shouts again. She shakes her head then sits up with a final yell. Her eyes are open, yet she feels like she is still dreaming. Jesse draws her knees to her chest and buries her head within them, tears flowing from her eyes. Aegis drops Kalup and goes over to sit next to the woman, wrapping a protective wing around her. Jesse leans against the Guardian, taking comfort as he wraps an arm around and hugs her.

"Jesse, what's wrong?" Nako asks.

"A bad dream, Nako. Just a really, really bad dream," Jesse answers.

"Bad dreams should not make you cry," Nako says as he tries to stand. He swears when his legs do not obey his commands.

"What the hell is going on?" Kalup demands, his words full of displeasure.

"I suggest, mortal, that you leave," Aegis warns the hotel tycoon. "Else you will end up joining the ranks of those below this crypt."

"You can't threaten me," Kalup says.

Aegis lowers his wing and stares at Kalup. Their gazes meet and the hotel tycoon swallows deeply before turning and leaving the room. Aegis nods firmly then returns his attention to Jesse. Her breathing has returned to a normal pace as she pulls herself together. She sits up and uses her shirttail to dry her eyes a little more then gets to her feet, making sure to keep her sore ankle firmly on the ground. Jesse takes a deep breath in then slowly lets it out as she refocuses on the task at hand.

"Where is Louis?" Jesse inquires.

"He decided to try and get Ronan to break into the system," Nako said. "Are you sure you are OK Jesse?"

"I'm fine, Nako," Jesse assures him as she scratches the seraph cat softly behind his ears. "I think it is high time we all got out of here."

"Agreed," Aegis stands next to her.

Jesse uses care to zip Nako back into the duffle bag with a gentle kiss on his forehead. The seraph cat purrs as Aegis lifts the bag and follows Jesse from the small room, closing the door behind. The entire room hushes when she makes her appearance. Jesse looks up when Louis makes a happy sound and hurries over to give her a dragon-bear hug. She smiles until she notices that the computer is still in its bag upon Louis's back. Jesse taps the Aligon on the shoulder to be released. He obliges her as she smiles up at him and then walks past him to scan the room in order to locate Ronan. She sees him trying to hide among The Faithful. Jesse approaches the group in order to speak with the young man. Aegis hands Nako to Louis and follows the woman.

Those protecting Ronan start to close ranks, forming a wall around the programmer. The Faithful then start chanting or singing a gospel song to keep the woman at bay. Jesse pauses a few feet from the people, crosses her arms and arches an eyebrow. Ronan hollers as he is lifted by an invisible force up and over the heads of his protectors. They stop singing and gasp in surprise as the young man turns upside down right above their heads. Jesse points to a wall and Ronan flies over and lands against it. His protectors rush forward but are sent back by a rush of wind from Aegis's wings. The Guardian crosses his arms and stares down the group of men.

"Do not be foolish," Aegis warns. The men hesitate and then move back to distance themselves from the Guardian.

"Ronan, why haven't you deactivated the hotel's systems and Ouija program by now?" Jesse asks as she approaches.

"Have you seen that computer? It's nothing more than a door-stop," Ronan responds. "That damn thing is not going to get on any network. It is worthless."

"So, you are reneging on your word," Jesse says, her voice trembling with anger. "My friends and I went through hell to get that computer. Nako nearly died."

"I don't care," Ronan interrupts. He gasps when a purple flame surrounds him, and are close enough to smolder his eye-brows.

"Irava is not the only one that can command a flame," Jesse leans closer to the programmer. "If you don't give at least a half-hearted try, I will personally feed you to the Nightmares that roam this cursed hotel."

"You don't know the hell that she promised for disobedience," Ronan whimpers.

"Do you wish to test me on that?" Jesse asks, well aware of the purple flames dancing in her eyes as she glares at the program-mer.

"N-no...Okay I will try..." Ronan says meekly.

"Good man," Jesse says and walks away from him.

Ronan grunts when he falls to the floor as Jesse releases him. She turns and watches him shrink back from her. The programmer wisely, and with nervous speed, approaches Louis to retrieve the computer. Ronan sits down with his back against the wall then opens and turns on the computer. It beeps and shows its BIOS screen before going into self-diagnosis. Louis sits down next to the programmer as the operating system comes up with a pleasant-sounding introduction. Ronan's jaw drops at the speed at which the computer powered up and the software that it has preloaded.

"Oh my God, where did you get this computer? It has the government's top secret hacker software on board," Ronan says in awe.

"Not so secret if you know about it," Louis counters. "Better get started before Jesse gets impatient."

Ronan glances over the laptop screen to see Jesse watching closely. He mutters as he averts his eyes back to his task at hand, typing frantically on the keyboard. Jesse takes a deep breath and turns away. She goes over to talk to Aegis in order to start discussing how they are going to get everyone out. She whips back around when she hears Ronan swear bitterly. The young man stands up and is about to toss the computer. Louis grabs the item before the programmer does the foolish deed and then glares at the young man.

"What happened?" Louis inquires.

"He locked me out, the son of a bitch," Ronan says as if offended. "I was almost there!"

"What network did you try?" Kalup inquires, standing a short distance from Jesse. "The guest network or the main one?"

"I tried forcing the main, the guest and the security networks," Ronan grumbles. "He has a firm hold on all three of them."

The rumbling of military bots catches Jesse's attention first. She turns to look out the door; the bots are moving much faster than the ones they ran into in the hotel. Three military transport bots, each with a portable No-Ghost tower, rumble into the cavern. The bots spread out into a formation as they erect the towers one at a time. Jesse decides that she does not like what she is witnessing and turns back to the room.

"Kalup, are there any other networks in this hotel?" Jesse inquires.

"Just my private network, which I will not disclose," Kalup shrugs. "Unless, of course, you are willing to provide a passionate exchange for it."

"My answer remains as always." Jesse said firmly. "What is the network, Kalup?"

The No-Ghost towers whirl and hiss as they come to life, their holographic lenses blinking as they warm up for operation. Jesse holds her ground as Kalup's features light up with a feral grin. He slides into her personal space, ignoring the Guardian standing a few feet away. Aegis crosses his arms as Kalup reaches to caress Jesse's cheek. She arches an eyebrow and stops his touch an inch from her form. Her eyes light up with purple flames as she figures out the code for the private network. Kalup gasps as he is picked up by the same forces that grabbed him in the gift shop and thrown towards a wall. He slams into it and slides down, holding his now-broken arm. Ronan swears but remains in place as Jesse turns to him.

"Ronan, look for OT50065," Jesse said.

"Here you go," Louis hands the computer back to the programmer.

"OT…" Ronan said as he types the name. "Found it, that's it! Looking for a password."

"It's Jesse Monroe," Jesse answers, a trickle of anger dripping from her words.

Ronan sits down to type in the password and makes a triumphant sound when he logs in. He skips past the images on the screen and activates the built-in program to attack the hotel's networks. Outside the church, the No-Ghost towers finish warming up and start to glow with an exceedingly bright light. A giant Ouija board appears to float from the ceiling and land upon the ground with a mighty thump.

The ground and church shake from the landing of the board, prompting Aegis to look outside. The board takes up the entire room, the bottom of which is at the gated entrance of the church. Strange symbols, different from the previous Ouija boards, light up and glow like fire. The board's giant planchette lowers from the darkness above, landing on it with a thump.

"Ronan, you need to hurry up," Aegis orders. "The creature that this board can bring forth is more powerful than I am."

Ronan concentrates on the screen as he clicks different items as prompted by the hacker's software. The people inside of the church all begin to whimper as the entire hotel vibrates from the movement of the giant planchette. Military bots start to drone in a humanlike voice as they chant a phrase over and over again. Christine seems to recognize the words and swears as she gets up and retreats to the back of the building. She rapidly draws a protective circle around herself and concentrates on her survival. Jesse whispers a prayer to the divine as she too recognizes the chant.

"Faster Ronan," Jesse urges.

The planchette moves sluggishly from one strange letter to another. Each time, the letter appears just above the board, spelling out a word or name. Ronan taps the enter key and the computer itself goes to work. The first thing to shut down is the emergency lights, followed closely by the guest network. The laptop hums, the processor increasing to the fullest capacity as it battles then shuts down the main network of the hotel and the old, currently unused, cellular network. The screen moves so fast that Ronan just stares as the computer does battle once again and deactivates the security network.

"Come on, come on," Louis encourages as he watches the screen as well.

The entire building quakes and heats up as the planchette slides bit by bit from one side of the board to the other in order to complete the summoning. The military bots increase the speed and volume of the chant as the word itself catches fire in the air. The laptop stops trying to force it one way and goes in an entirely different route, the old cellular network, all on its own. The building stops quaking as the laptop's fans begin to decrease in volume.

The military bot's last words echo into the hotel, but none follow it. The No-Ghost towers all shut down and the Ouija board as well as the words in the air disappear. The camera network goes blank, and the main computers of the hotel shut completely down, ending the program. In the hotel beyond the church, every single robot drops to the floor and becomes lifeless. The main lights of the hotel pop on, illuminating the darkened space. Jesse decides to walk bravely into the cavern just beyond the church's stoop but stops short of going beyond the graves. She exhales in relief when she sees that the three military bots do not react to her presence, and that they have all been deactivated.

"Holy shit! I did it!" Ronan crows. "I beat Charlie! The Ouija program is deactivated."

"I wish you had not proclaimed that so quickly, Ronan," Jesse says with a shake of her head.

The sound of struggling is heard right before five people run out the church. Jesse jumps to the side to clear the path as the people run, full speed, to the hall that leads to the vendor hall and ultimately outside. As soon as the five go beyond the church's fence they are attacked, viciously, by the asylum ghosts. A couple of them manage to dodge the first wave of specters and continue to the hall. Their escape is temporary when they are eaten whole by a cat-snake. It hisses a chuckle as it once again turns invisible. A second group of people hesitate at the church's door when they witness the massacre. They then retreat into the building and huddle in the corner furthest from the door. Jesse takes a deep breath in as she turns and walks back into the church.

"You lying, deceiving, witch!" The Faithful leader shouts, his words ripe with outrage.

"Excuse me?" Jesse arches an eyebrow and faces the man.

"You told us that once the program is deactivated, the ghosts would be gone. Oh, woe to us for believing such lies!" The man continues. Several more people also shout at Jesse, hurling very unpleasant words upon at the woman.

"Silence!" Aegis shouts over the noise. "That is not what I heard. What we all heard."

"The conversation that you overheard me having with the PIU officer was this," Jesse turns to face the room. "The Ouija program needed to be deactivated so that it would not bring forth any more spirits into the hotel. Those spirits that are already here would then be our concern. There are a variety of ghosts and other demons all waiting for us to run blindly into their trap."

"The trap that you laid," The Faithful leader accuses in anger. "You are the one orchestrating the attacks on us! You and your demon spawn are responsible for it all!"

"You place the blame on the wrong woman, bastard," Jesse addresses. "We need to make a plan for those willing to leave this place to follow. Before that, I need to talk to you in private, Aegis."

"Why not have the conversation so we all can hear it," Kalup demands as he cradles his broken arm.

"Because it does not concern you or anyone else," Jesse retorts. She looks up at Aegis and continues to the room at the back of the stage.

Jesse massages her temples as she walks into the room. Aegis closes the door behind them and takes a couple of steps beyond. He stands there and waits as Jesse paces back and forth, trying to figure out where to start. She stops pacing and faces the Guardian, focusing on his now-calm-steel-blue eyes.

"Let me start by saying thank you for assisting us out of this place," Jesse said. "I wanted to talk to you because this is our final hour, and there are no guarantees."

"As I said previously, you are the only Spell Caster willing to find a way to get every ungrateful mortal out of this hotel that you can," Aegis responds. "I want to assist you. Besides, you remind me of someone special to me."

"Jessica," Jesse nods at his reaction. "Yes, I met her while I was asleep. She told me that she is half of the energies keeping this church from being overrun by ghosts and spirits."

"Half?" Aegis asks.

"She gave me a warning that her powers are fading, and we need to get out as soon as possible," Jesse continues. "She was also highly concerned about the Mistress of the Flames. I had a nightmare about that too."

"The clues of the Mistress's presence are everywhere," Aegis says. "I just have to find and dispose of her."

"Her name is Irava," Jesse answers. "I think Kalup and Ronan are her retainers. Jessica and I talked about this, she even asked me to give you a message," Jesse takes a deep breath as she formulates the words. "She said that she loves you and that they forgave you long ago."

"They? No one else was there when Jessica died, as far as I know," Aegis tilts his head in curiosity.

"Now the coup de grace," Jesse mutters to herself, then takes a deep breath and looks Aegis in the eyes. "Jessica showed me how she died. She neglected to tell you that she was pregnant when she was attacked by the Flames of Madness."

The shock upon the Guardian's face speaks volumes upon hearing the news. Aegis closes his eyes, his body trembles as he fights to control a powerful rage. Jesse takes a couple of steps back until the large concrete table she slept on is between them.

Aegis' wings fold back in slow motion and start quivering. The small church also vibrates as Jesse mumbles under her breath. She should have taken position near the door. Aegis tilts his head back and unleashes a bellow of pure rage as he disappears in a shower of lightning bolts. Jesse takes advantage of his absence and leave the room.

"What happened?" Nako asks as Jesse reaches his side.

"Gave Aegis a message from the past," Jesse answers.

"Will he be calm enough to help us?" Louis asks.

"I hope so," Jesse says.

Aegis reappears in front of the window at the rear of the church. Christine swears and makes herself scarce when she senses the angry energy coming from the Guardian. Aegis sneers at the depiction of the beast before he punches the window. It shatters with one hit, falling to the floor. Aegis lands as the shards start to take on a golden glow.

The debris levitates and begins to coalesce upon Aegis's body. A bright glow blinds everybody in the room, many of the refugees scream in fear. The light dies down allowing Jesse to lower her hand as she takes in the fully armed Guardian standing on the stage. The window has repaired itself but no longer shows the two opponents. Instead, it shows the beast by itself impaled upon an overly large sword. The shaky breathing of the Guardian breaks the silence of the hall. Jesse bravely approaches him.

"Aegis," Jesse stops a short distance from the Guardian. "Apologies, perhaps I should have waited until we were out of here."

"I..." Aegis takes a deep breath. "Your timing is fine, Jesse. Once you and your friends are free of this place, I have a hunt. We leave in orderly fashion."

"I will line up those that are willing to go," Jesse nods and turns.

"Jesse," Aegis says causing the woman to face him again. "What was the child's name?"

"Her name was Anna," Jesse answers.

Jesse walks away from the Guardian and calls for the attention of those in the church. She starts giving orders about how to line up. Christine frowns when she hears her position in the line. Louis wisely packs up the laptop and slings it onto his back then picks up Nako, duffle bag and all. The seraph cat mews in pain, but it is not as bad as before. Jesse sees that all but a handful of people are eager to go. She turns and tries not to react unfavorably as she faces The Faithful.

"Don't even look this way, devil witch," The Faithful leader commands. "We are not going to line up so that your demons can pick us off. We are staying in this sanctuary, where it is safe."

"Okay," Jesse shrugs and walks to the front of the line. "We are moving out, quietly."

"Angel, will you not stay?" The Faithful leader beseeches of the Guardian. "We are the LORD's sheep. We need your protection more than the ones that turn their back on HIM."

"You are indeed sheep," Aegis agrees. "I suggest you join the herd that is being led by a lioness to secure your safe passage out of this place."

The refugees huddle together as they walk from the safe confines of the church and into the great unknown. Aegis waits until the last of them is headed out the door before he starts to follow. Those left behind start to whisper among themselves but are silenced by their leader. Kalup decides to stay with The Faithful to avoid the Guardian and the fate which awaits the evacuees. The crowd gathers just prior to the fence as Jesse looks about, noting the mechanical carnage in the hall. She once again makes sure that the towers are not activated before she places a hand on the gate.

"We are going straight to the front door," Jesse said. "We might run into the PIU on the way."

"Hope to run into them," Louis offers.

"Speak for yourself, dragon boy," Christine grumbles.

"I will stay towards the center of the group and pass the word of our destination," Louis ignores the woman.

The gate squeaks as Jesse opens it and steps out into the massive room. The determined group of refugees follow in her footsteps, walking in a straight line to the hall leading to the vendor areas. More than one evacuee marvels at the destroyed military bots and disabled transport bots still in the room. Jesse continues into the hall, ignoring the giant sawblade that is half buried into the wall above.

Halfway down the hall, Jesse swears as a group of asylum ghosts appear and attack. They smash into an invisible barrier and destroy themselves. Christine jumps and swears when she sees the lights, amazed that no one is being killed. A cat-snake demon appears in front of the group. It rears up to attack then falls apart into three pieces, each disintegrating upon hitting the floor. Aegis appears briefly, then turns and disappears as he goes after another attacker.

Jesse wisely increases the pace through the tunnel while the Guardian continues to work. Lights buzz as the refugees walk deeper into the hallway. A dozen or more apparitions float about observing the living and seem humored by their presence. The ghosts then dissipate into a white haze that is filling the entire hotel. Jesse pauses when the nurse ghost shows up, grins, then disappears into the white haze.

Gospel hymns rise up, stemming from the church. Jesse and the evacuees stop when they hear the distance noise. The lead shakes her head as she calls for those with her to continue down the path. Aegis pauses when he hears them, as do many of the stronger ghouls he is facing. The ghosts disappear, leaving Aegis in a state of mild shock. The hymns soon turn to shrieks of terror as the ghosts enter the church, undeterred and attack The Faithful. Aegis straightens his stance with a solemn look on his face. He then turns and disappears, once again taking up position with Jesse's group.

Jesse and the evacuees exit the hall into the massive vendor area. She hesitates in her stride when she notices each and every vendor booth is set up, nothing broken or missing. Anything that was previously trampled upon or destroyed is now in pristine condition. She shakes her head, knowing for fact that this is not the way she left the space.

Louis looks around and finds a booth that he personally smashed into when they outran a military bot. It looks pristine as if nothing happened to it. The tunnel they ran down is still destroyed. Many of the refugees appear to be entranced by the sparkling of the various jewels and trinkets left unguarded. The light in the vendor area is bright, as if to highlight the most valuable of items. Jesse glances about then focus her concentration on leading the evacuees to the door that leads outside.

The steel riot doors are now open with the glass doors a lobby length beyond. The fog thickens as the group slows down. It soon becomes so thick that it is hard to see. Jesse barely sees a woman in front of her take a left and decides to follow. Christine does the same. Louis pauses when he notices many of the people have stopped walking and stare into the room. He turns and frowns when he sees strange spirits floating around, playing within the mist. The figure of a woman forms, unnoticed by many, then dissipates.

"What's going on?" Louis inquires. He looks around and frowns. "Where's Jesse?"

"She's missing?" Nako asks and scans the area. "Christine's not here either."

"What are you waiting for?" a female voice echoes in the entire room. "Such treasures, such sparkle. It would be a waste to let all of this go. No one is guarding it, why don't you indulge?"

"Oh my God, it's Irava," Ronan said, his voice quaking with fear. "We have to run!"

The programmer bolts to the door as a few refugees decide to trek into the vendor hall and sift through the unguarded booths. More follow as they become brave or curious enough to do so. Louis calls for the attention of the refugees and follows the programmer on his quick retreat to the door. Over half of the evacuees follow him, jogging through the fog. The pillagers continue their spree, oblivious that their friends are leaving them. Jewelry cases are smashed as the looting picks up to near fever pitch. Fights break out among them for a special piece that more than one person wants.

A snapping sound echoes in the room. The fog ignites into flames, catching all by surprise. Those caught by the flame scream in pain at first, then start to laugh in uncontrollable madness. The ones being consumed by the flames attack any living being near them, bringing the victims into the insanity. Louis slides to a stop, finding himself surrounded by the strange laughing fire. He glares at the obstacle as he tucks Nako under one arm. A cold wind blows the fire out around the Aligon as Aegis appears with sword drawn.

"Where is Jesse?" Aegis demands.

"Don't know, she disappeared before the flames started," Louis answers. "There was a thick fog with strange faces then Irava convinced some of the refugees to wander into the room."

"Irava is the Mistress of the Flames of Madness," Aegis informs Louis. "I will see if I can find Jesse then deal with the Mistress. Are you able to speed your way out of here?"

"I am not a track star, but I can run faster than most humans," Louis offers.

"Then get going," Aegis says firmly.

The Guardian faces the way out and swings his sword with a mighty yell. The wind arches out from the blade and extinguishes flames down the path. Louis starts running, getting up to speed as he chases the wind. Aegis disappears as Louis reaches the stairs going up into the lobby. The Aligon curses as he slides to a stop, taking a couple of hops back so that he distances himself from a new obstacle.

A large pack of ghostly security dogs, accompanied by their ghoulish handlers, stand between the living and the exit door. Louis glances around to see that around twenty refugees are also facing the exit and Ronan is nowhere in sight. He turns and see several strange creatures stalking up the stairs, followed by the Flames of Madness as those being consumed by it make their way to the exit. The sound of several people gasping brings the Aligon's attention back to the obstacle in front of them.

There is now a shimmering golden shadow of a woman just inside the doors. She lifts her hand and places two fingers just beyond her lips. A high pitch whistle comes from the woman causing Nako to lift his head and the guard dogs to turn. Seconds later a large pack of silver hounds spring from just beyond the glass and attack their ghostly counterparts. The guards themselves are mowed down by a barrage of silver arrows, disappearing as they hit the ground. The glass just beyond the rescuer shatters, raining down to reveal the outside as a second figure enters the space.

"Everybody, get out, now!" Diana shouts to the masses.

The refugees are spurred by her words and run towards the shattered glass beyond the rescuers. A group of ghoul's rush forward to indulge in a feast of the living. Their charge is cut short when they hit an invisible barrier and freeze in place. Deloris calmly floats down from a short distance above with her arms crossed. The vampress points the palm of her hand at the frozen attackers and says two words. The fiends yowl as their bodies turns white then crumble into dust.

Deloris lands on the ground with a smile of confidence upon her features. She turns to talk to her companions as the flames rush into the invisible barrier. Deloris stumbles forward then turns to see what hit her shield. The flames slam into it again, knocking Deloris onto her backside. The flames wrap around as much of the barrier as it can, licking its way to the top. Diana sees what is happening then looks up and locks onto a sprinkler head just above the flames. It is still dormant, perhaps deactivated when the rest of the networks went down. Diana decides to figure it out later as she aims her pistol at the sprinkler. Her Aethoes also aims at the item, drawing back her bow. Both fire at the same time with the bullet hitting the release for the sprinkler.

It rains down on the flames as the arrow sails past the target and obliterates a device just beyond the sprinkler. The entire vendor room and lobby area sprinkling system activates, pouring water all over the flames and those on fire. The flames cry out in agony as the liquid douses them. The burning victims, still alive, scream as water washes over them then pass out or start muttering incoherently.

"What was that thing?" Diana asks.

"Flames of Madness," Louis answers as he approaches the officers. "The Mistress of which is still inside."

"What happened to Sir Nako?" Deloris inquires, noticing the wounded cat.

"He was attacked by a ghost dog while retrieving the computer that helped free us," Louis replies and lifts the backpack with his tail.

"Where is Ms. Monroe?" Diana asks.

"Don't know, she was with the group when we started out then disappeared when the thick fog rolled in," Louis responds. "Christine Longstraw is also missing, I'm not sure where they are."

"Artemis and I are going in to look for them," Diana announces.

"This place is very dangerous," Louis warns. "Even though we deactivated the software for now, it may be a matter of time before Charlie figures out how to bring it up again."

"Can you give the computer to Officer Moody on your way out, Dr. Lygtbut?" Deloris requests.

"Of course," Louis nods.

"Be careful, all of you," Nako said as Louis turns and leaves the hotel.

As soon as the Aligon leaves the lobby, the sound of robots coming online echoes throughout the entire hotel. The lobby bots booted up into security mode, calling for the hotel security to assist with the intruders Diana arches an eyebrow as she puts her weapon away. She crosses her arms as an energy wave washes over the entire lobby and vending hall. All mechanical activity short circuits and shuts down. Diana then follows her Aethoes and Deloris into the vendor hall and looks about.

The entire place is in ruin from the looting activity. Bodies, both burned and decapitated, are scattered throughout the floor. Artemis decides to go into a left passageway as Diana and Deloris head down a main tunnel towards the church. The path to get to the small building is undeterred, many of the specters that once roamed it are now gone thanks to Aegis.

The smell of fresh blood permeates Deloris's senses. Diana pauses outside at her senior officer's request to allow Deloris to go in by herself. The scene she enters is straight out of a horror movie with dismembered body parts as well as blood and gore everywhere. Deloris glances around when she hears the heartbeat of a survivor. She follows the sound until she gets to the church's office and opens the door.

"Don't come any closer," Kalup shouts, obviously frightened, as he holds up a large iron cross.

"I suggest you put the makeshift weapon down," Deloris retorts. "I also need for you to identify yourself."

"I am Kalup Leyman, owner of this hotel. I was awaiting assistance with a large group of people when the ghosts attacked," Kalup says. "What of Jesse and those who left, did they survive or were they killed?"

"Mixed bag. But we will go into details later," Deloris answers. "I myself am curious to know how you survived an obvious massacre."

"I...can't really answer that," Kalup admits. "I don't know."

"Hmm..." Deloris considers his answer. "We will talk more later, Mr. Leyman. Right now, let us get out of here before I do something I may regret."

Deloris leaves the room first as Kalup watches her go. He smiles, admiring her features then jumps when he hears someone behind him. Turning, the tycoon takes a couple of steps back when he sees a ghostly image of Irava. She winks at him then disappears. Kalup hurries after the PIU officer.

CHAPTER NINE

Mistress of the Flame

The silence of the hall is interrupted by the noise of mechanical systems coming back online. Christine grumbles as she boldly walks down the middle of the corridor in search of an exit. She pauses by a digital map as it lights back up, indicating the area where she is currently. She gawks when she sees that she is on the 150th floor of the hotel. Christine takes in her surroundings and frown, not sure what to make of the lighting and the environment. It reminds her of a child's book with the vivid colors and painted figures.

"How in the world did I get here," Christine asks herself, dumbfounded. "This is ridiculous, maybe I should have stayed with the religious fanatics."

The clopping of horse's hooves upon the floor brings Christine's attention to the corner she had just rounded. The floor shakes as a large coal black stallion walk, unhurried, into the light. He has red eyes and flames exiting his nostrils. The fire makes a giggling sound as it spirals around his head. The stallion takes a few more steps into the hall, revealing he has a headless rider upon his back. Christine swears as she takes a step backwards. The headless rider reaches behind and pulls out a flaming horseman's axe. The fire upon the blade snickers as if it has heard an inside joke. To Christine's surprise, laughter also comes from both the horse and its rider.

"Has everything gone mad here?" Christine stresses out loud.

The stallion rears up, charging forward as the rider swings his axe and cackles with glee. Christine drops some unfiltered words as she erects a barrier between herself and the attacking creatures. She holds her ground as the attacker slams into the shield. The horse kicks it a few times then bursts into flames. The fire laughs as it licks up to the top of the barrier, close to the ceiling but does not catch it on fire.

"Why the hell aren't the sprinklers working?" Christine sneers.

The flames reshape to form a combination of the rider with a horse's head and hind legs as he uses a larger axe to chop into the barrier. Christine stands her ground as she starts motioning with her arms. The spell she is casting cascades from her lips. The shield breaks as the last words fall. The horseman bellows as he attacks, swinging his axe to take the woman's head. His arm and blade are pulled strongly to a center of intense supernatural gravity as a dark portal opens in front of the woman. It pulls, harshly, upon the horseman, sucking the entire specter into the portal before slamming shut. Christine tosses her hair as she smiles confidently at the empty space.

"When I get out of here, I am going to sue the hell out of this place," Christine muses to herself.

The lights buzz as Christine walks leaves the scene, heading down the hall towards an elevator shaft. Giggling behind makes her pause in her step. A sneer creases her lip as she turns to face her follower. Her anger turns to outright terror when she sees the strange beast with flames licking at its lips. The giggling is coming from the fire itself. The beast blinks and grins menacingly at Christine.

"Oh, hell no," Christine says and runs away from the beast.

The Beast of the Flames trots after her then unleashes the flames as Christine makes it to a staircase. The PIU officer opens the door and slams it shut before immediately drawing a symbol upon the dust on the window. The flames hit the door but do not burst through immediately. Christine takes a couple of steps back then does a panicked run down the stairs as the flames break down the door. The beast's laughter echoes in the stairwell as it gives chase.

The emergency lights illuminate the way down the twilight hall. Jesse swears as she limps into a large open room. The space is void of any furniture, showing off the nice marble floors. Jesse searches the room and takes in the surroundings to include several painted windows that simulate two-tone stained-glass. A large edifice of a cross is on the wall opposite the entrance. It looks to be standing on a rotating carousel with the back against a false wall. Jesse approaches the cross and takes note of the button on the floor. She steps on it.

There is a loud mechanical click as a hidden lever is lifted. The wall rotates as a weight fall and stops on an idol of a woman with child. Jesse steps on another button on the floor and the statue rotates up, using a similar mechanism, and stops on a statue of a man sitting in meditation. It then drifts to the left to another man with four arms and an elephant's head. The drift continues through various other deities and even flips up once again to a third carousel. Jesse frowns until she notices that she is still stepping on the button. She releases her hold, and the carousel stops on an abstract statue of a goddess.

"Let's see, I don't see any ghosts or obstacles around. The statues did not come to life," Jesse says, searching the room. "Since I've somehow gotten myself lost, let me see if I can invoke some assistance."

Jesse sits down in a corner of the room, out of sight. After another quick look around, she unties her bag of trinkets and pulls out a small box of old-fashioned crayons. Jesse smiles as she takes out her favorite color among the fat sticks of colored wax; purple. She places the crayon on its tip and taps the end of it.

The crayon moves by itself, drawing a circle around Jesse and a few other symbols as she removes the trinkets from the bag. The crayon finishes drawing a perfect triangle in front of her then jumps back into the box. Jesse places the necklace at the top of the triangle, the bracelet to the right and the broach on the left. She then inhales deeply, closing her eyes to concentrate.

Elsewhere in the hotel's darkened galleries, an eerie silvery light chases away the shadows as a figure traverse down the passageway. Artemis looks around, noting the spirits of the departed. They range in age, era when they died, and sanity.

Artemis rounds a corner and freezes in place when a strange, yet familiar feeling overtakes her. Curiosity masks her features as she turns to face the way she had just come. She hears a voice softly speaking as the person reaches out to her. Artemis lifts her free hand as a ball of light hovers just above her palm.

Back inside of the multi-worship room, the purple crayon marks on the floor change to silver and start to glow. Jesse opens her eyes and calms her first reaction upon seeing the change. The trinkets pulsate as the space in the middle of the triangle takes on a brilliant silver glow, almost like a mirror. Jesse investigates it and gasps when a pair of blue-green eyes stare back at her.

"Greetings Artemis," Jesse nods respectfully.

"Jesse?" Artemis responds as the eyes reflect her recognition. "Where are you?"

"I don't know," Jesse answers truthfully. "I am in a multi-religion room right now. Still trying to figure out how I got to the floor."

"I see," Artemis said. Her eyes cut to the left, briefly. "Stay put, I will be there after a minor skirmish."

"Okay." Jesse says.

The circle goes back to crayon purple, but the trinkets continue to pulsate. Jesse frowns as she picks up the bracelet. It disappears out of her hand, stunning her momentarily, then reappears on her right arm. The broach is pinned to the right side of her shirt and the necklace is now proudly hanging from her neckline. Jesse exhales in relief as she settles down to await assistance.

The doors to the room burst open as Christine runs into the space. She slams the doors close and hastily draws a very powerful seal upon them. Jesse comes to her feet as the creature that pursued the PIU officer slams into the door. Christine backs away as the door starts to heat up, glowing an angry shade of orange.

"What's happening?" Jesse asks.

"You better run if you don't want to end up toast," Christine responds.

With that, Christine turns and runs for the back of the room. She pushes on the statue and squeezes through the opening it provides. Jesse swears as small flames giggle as they lick through the crack at the top of the door. She grits her teeth and moves as fast as she can to the statue and follows Christine. The wall flips automatically to the next statue as the doors melt away. Irava saunters into the room with an evil smile upon her lips.

The hallway that Jesse finds herself in is dark at first then starts to light up as mechanical and lighting systems come back online. Red lights twinkle in the twilight of the hall, warning the women that they are in a service passageway. The lighting upon the various statues gives the illusion that they are watching the passage of the unintended guests. Jesse notes the door ahead of her and sees that it is ajar. She hesitates a moment then makes the decision to go into the room after the PIU officer.

The normally Artic air is excessively hot as several computers hum and beep as they come up online at full tilt. Jesse sees Christine standing not too far from the door where they had both entered the space, her jaw agape with awe. The keys upon the holographic keyboard on the large mainframes light up rhythmically as invisible hands frantically type in commands.

"Where is this place?" Jesse frowns.

"Hell if I know, do I look like a geek?" Christine demands. "I'm just looking for a way out."

"I don't have time for your spoiled, selfish, attitude," Jesse said through gritted teeth. Her next thought pauses as the room takes on a large shadow. She looks up and stares. "Oh, my word..."

A Ouija board the size of a conference table floats down and lands upon the floor with an audible thump. A glowing pentagram spins underneath it as the planchette falls from above and lands upon the board with a distinctive wooden noise. All the computers in the room whistle as they reach the highest speeds possible, at least two of them heading into overload as smoke starts to fill the room. Christine edges away from Jesse as she backs to the door.

The PIU officer lets out a scream of surprise as she is hoisted up into the air, catching Jesse's attention. Jesse jumps back and shields herself from an invisible weapon. She casts a reveal spell soon after making the entire room pulsate and tint blue. Charlie grins at the woman before sending his belts after her again. Jesse swears and dodges the first few times. Her luck runs out as Charlie captures her by the waist and hoist her up into the air. She gags as she feels him squeezing her, as if trying to slice her in half. Jesse reaches into her back pocket and pulls the Dragon Tarot's Fool card and tosses it at her attacker.

The card explodes into a scrawny silver dragon, roaring as he attacks the ghost. Charlie drops his prey in surprise as the dragon charges toward him. The dragon goes through the ghost and lands on the main computer in the room, digging his claws in and tearing it apart. Smoke and strange noises erupt from the machine as the dragon turns back into a card and returns to Jesse's hand. She stands up as one by one the rest of the machine shuts down. The Ouija board fades from the room before it can begin any summoning. Christine swears as she gets to her feet.

Charlie bellows, infuriated, as he launches his belts toward Jesse. She swiftly picks up a floor tile and causes it to glow purple, holding it tight as the belts slap into the item. The weapons bounce off then tries to reach the woman by going around the tile, but are too short to touch her. Charlie sneers then bellows as he unleashes an energy wave.

Jesse braces as it slams into her then loses her footing and is sent backwards. She stops when she hits Christine, then both hit the wall. They are held against it as Jesse drops unladylike words and Christine makes a sound that her companion has never heard before. The energy field holding the two drops, sending them to the floor. Both stand and face the room.

"What do we do?" Christine inquires, slight annoyance in her words.

"We?" Jesse repeats, stunned by the words. "Are you alright?"

"That idiot dared to touch me, I want to send him to the furthest region of hell that exists," Christine sneers as a green whirl of energy roars to life around her.

"Where was this attitude an hour ago?" Jesse pulls out her old Tarot deck.

Jesse sifts through her deck and pulls out the Eight of Swords as Charlie goes over to one of the machines and gets it going again. It coughs and sputters as Jesse pulls out a second card,

Strength. The Ouija program starts up with the planchette moving frantically to spell out a forbidden name. It freezes as Jesse releases her cards; several swords appear around Charlie, stabbing into the Ouija board.

Rope extends from the handles and wraps around the wraith, locking him in place. The lights turn a concerning shade of red as Christine begins her chant. The smell of fresh blood fills the room as a wave of darkness washes over the entire area. Jesse glances over at Christine when she hears the rare and dangerous incantation.

"I hope you know what you are doing," Jesse says aloud.

The Ouija board pulsates between blue and green lights before going red as Christine concentrates. Charlie howls in surprise and fear as he begins to sink down into the board. The computer he brought up wheezes then dies? The Ouija board fades away as the swords disappear, once again becoming the two separate cards.

Jesse swears and takes hold of the cards. She is about to recast them when Charlie cheers his freedom and immediately jumps into a secondary machine before it completely shuts down. Christine cancels her spell and turns to light into Jesse for letting the ghoul go. Instead, she freezes when she notices a previously undetected presence in the room.

"I am impressed, no one has cast that particular spell in generations," Irava says to Christine. Jesse faces the woman.

"You've not seen anything yet. How do I get out of this hell-hole?" Christine demands.

"There are a few ways, do you wish to take the easy way out?" Irava inquires with a grin.

"I don't like this," Jesse says. She makes her way backwards to the door.

"If you direct me to the nearest window, I'll let myself out," Christine said.

Jesse with practiced speed and stealth, slips through the door as Irava grins maliciously at Christine. Flames roar to life behind the woman as the PIU officer curses up a storm. The flames giggle as Irava directs them in Christine. The PIU officer stumbles backward when the fire launches in her direction.

Christine screams as she runs through the door and slams it behind her. Jesse looks back when she hears the noise. She curses before she picks up her own pace and runs through the statues back to the multi-religious room. Jesse is first to exit into the room followed closely by Christine.

The two manage to stop to avoid running into a wall of cackling fire. Jesse whips around and notices that the fire that chased Christine is now blocking the escape route. Christine shrieks, catching Jesse's attention. The flames blocking the main door launch towards them gleefully. They make a squeal like noise when they slam into an invisible shield. Jesse strains as the fire wraps around the shield and beats upon it. She falls to her knees with the strain of keeping the attacker at bay as Irava walks through the fire and smiles, crossing her arms.

"It seems that we have a very familiar situation," Irava said. "You will not last long, mortal."

"Christine, snap out of it, I need help," Jesse says through grit teeth. Her pleas fall on deaf ears. Christine seems to be stunned at her situation, rocking back and forth like a terrified child.

"Let's play a game, shall we?" Irava announces.

"Let's not," Jesse manages.

The flames form into a large sledgehammer and slam on the shield harshly. Jesse bucks but remains strong. The fire laughs hysterically and once again hit the obstacle; a crack forms, much to Jesse's dismay. The fiery hammer lifts once more and comes down to deliver the final blow. A strong, cold, wind blows into the room and fills it with an artic chill.

The entire area extinguishes with ice replacing the flames, caking onto the walls. Irava appears stunned at first then turns in time for a strong force to slam into her, sending her into the wall next to the rotating statues. Aegis fades into view standing between Jesse and the threat. He draws his weapon in preparation of the coming battle. The shield around Jesse shatters as it collapses and she places her hands upon the ground. She manages to catch her breath as she looks up.

"Aegis, I am so happy to see you," Jesse says.

"I found you as fast as I could," Aegis assures her as he helps her to her feet. "This hotel is the Mistress's playground. She and her minions can manipulate it at will. Remember that as you find your way out."

"You're not coming with us?" Christine asks, astonished, as she gets to her feet.

"No," Aegis says. "My business is with Irava tonight."

"I pray you are victorious, Aegis," Jesse says to the Guardian. "Come on, Christine. Maybe we can meet up with Artemis on the way out and all of us can escape this labyrinth."

"Meet up with who? I...think I'll stay here instead," Christine muses.

"Suit yourself," Jesse shrugs.

Flames burst from the hole in the wall as the room begins to quake. Thunder echoes in the hotel as Aegis spreads his wings, his sword lighting up with electric fury. Jesse did not stay to watch Irava exit the wall as she hurries into the hall. Christine swears under her breath when she notices that Irava is covered in flames, her eyes glowing orange with maddened rage.

Christine rapidly retreats for a few feet then turn and runs out the door in full tilt. Jesse limps down the hallway, following the green lights that point towards the exit when she hears rushing feet behind her. She turns in time to be slammed by Christine. Both women hit the ground with Jesse feeling her fragile ankle pop painfully. She swears bitterly and holds her leg as she tries to control the tremble of agony racking through her body.

Flames scream from the doorway and whip around after the women. Hysterical laughter as well as a roar emits from the fire as it comes down the hall. Christine lets out a sharp gasp as she stands up and runs in the direction opposite of the fire. Jesse glances back and tries to get to her feet.

The pain hits her, hard, knocking her back to the ground. The flames launch toward Jesse and hit a powerful invisible barrier just inches from her. They scream in anger as they beat against it, desperately searching for a weak spot. Not far down the hall, Christine curses and slides to a stop before she collides with another woman. The officer takes several hurried steps back from the new obstacle then finds that she is unable to move any further.

"So much for staying put," the woman said. Jesse stares at the woman as she approaches.

"Artemis," Jesse nods as she tries to stand. She immediately went back down. "Yea, I'm not walking or running anywhere?"

Jesse manages to get back on her feet and holds up the leg that is injured as the Chariot tarot card from her old deck appears in her hand. The building starts to rumble as she holds the card overhead a moment then tosses it in the air above her. The card bursts into a rain of golden dust.

A toga wraps around Jesse as a large, shining, golden chariot appears to rise from the ground underneath her. Two sphinxes, half man and half lion, appear hitched to the front of the vehicle. Jesse shifts her weight in order to comfortably place her sore foot down as she takes up the reins. The shaking becomes more violent as a new rush of flames and lightning streak down the hall and slam into the shield.

"Nice chariot," Artemis offers her complements.

"Thank you," Jesse acknowledges. "I'll come over to let you board."

"Actually, you need to get a running start," Artemis corrects her. "Once I lower the barrier, those flames will be after you,"

"What about Christine?" Jesse asks.

"What about her?" Artemis asks, shrugging.

"Respectfully, I think we should take her with us considering that if the flames consume her, Irava will have access to some very ancient and powerful dark magic," Jesse says.

"Really?" Artemis glances at Christine then turns her attention back to Jesse when the flames slam into the shield again. "Alright, come at me."

"Chaos, Harmony," Jesse speaks to the sphinxes as she picks up the lash. "Let's go, HA!"

Jesse cracks the whip and the twin sphinxes roar as they lunge forward, ramping up to full speed within a couple of steps. Christine mumbles a sailor's oath as she levitates off the floor. Artemis grins mischievously as she jumps and flips over the sphinx. She lands on the chariot right behind Jesse. Christine swears when she is placed to one side of the chariot. She holds onto the vehicle as it increases speed substantially.

The shield shatters and the flames launch after the chariot, cackling in glee from the chase. Artemis takes aim at a sprinkler head as they ride past it and releases her arrow. The bolt sails true and slams into the target. Water explodes from the sprinkler, pouring on the flames. The fire shrieks as they are knocked back. The effects do not last long as the flames regather just beyond the water and continue the pursuit. Artemis scowls at the flames and puts her bow away for the moment.

"Jesse, what cards do we use to combat these flames?" Artemis inquires.

"Um," Jesse said as she pulls on the reins to do a hard left. "Ace of Cups, Full Moon, Tempest and either the Star or the Queen of Cups will make a tidal wave."

"Okay where's the deck?" Artemis asks.

"My old deck is in my left jacket pocket. The novelty Dragon deck is in my back pocket but is not as reliable," Jesse says.

"Got it," Artemis pulls the old deck and sifts through the cards. "Why not both Queen and Star?"

"They don't get along," Jesse answers.

"Are you kidding me, you are actually having a conversation?" Christine interrupts. "The fire is getting closer!"

"At least your observation skills are not lacking, mortal," Artemis observes of Christine.

Jesse cracks the whip again to gain more speed from the sphinxes while Artemis pulls out all but the Queen of Cups and tosses them into the air. The space just behind the speeding chariot goes blank as a large orb descends upon the hall. The haunting glow seems to brighten as it receives outside influence from the summoner. A giant goblet full to the brim appears as well as two distinctively different women.

Together they tilt over the cup, spilling all the contents. The liquid swells up, filling up the entire hall, and rushes toward the flames. The fire seems to pause right before it is hit by the water. Steam and screams fill the hall, and all dissipate as the cards return to the deck. Jesse glances behind to see the result then her full attention goes to the front. A large group of ghost security hounds appear a distance away, yet they are steadily coming closer as the chariot speeds in their direction.

"Ghost dogs and security ahead," Jesse announces. "The Sun and all four Knights will give you a Calvary charge."

Artemis pulls the cards and puts them in motion. A shining white horse appears first at a full gallop and is immediately followed by four rambunctious knights, two on either side of the first horse. Artemis presses her fingers to her lips and releases a sharp whistle. A pack of silver hounds materialize from the darkness and run with the knights toward the enemy.

The attack is brief, and the cards return to the deck. A wall appears in front of them causing Jesse to swear again and pull on the reins. Christine shrieks in fear and holds on for dear life as the chariot takes a hard right. Artemis holds on as well then looks in front and behind; they are going the wrong direction to get outside.

"What happened?" Artemis asks.

"A wall appeared out of nowhere," Jesse answers. "Aegis warned me that the Mistress of the Flames of Madness and her minions have control over the hotel. Apparently, that means moving walls at will."

"Next time we come across a wall, we are going through it," Artemis says, retrieving the novelty Dragon Tarot cards from Jesse's back pocket.

Jesse barely hears the words as she feels a burning sensation light up the left side of her body. She looks down at her hand and sees the nerves within alit with a yellow glow. The glow travels up her arm and is on her neck and down to the wounded ankle.

Jesse's vision blurs slightly causing her to clear her head with a little shake. She whistles and cracks the whip once more to encourages the sphinxes to go faster. She makes sure to keep the reins straight and not veer from the path. The twin beasts roar as they obey the command.

A wall looms ahead, rapidly coming closer. Jesse cracks the whip again as another wall appears out of nowhere a few feet in front of them. Artemis unleashes the Dragon Page of Swords in front of the charging Chariot. The card explodes with a roar as an enormous green dragon gallop with his head down and wings folded firmly against his body. He reaches ramming speed and goes through the first wall. Jesse directs the sphinxes to follow as close to the edge of the tail of the dragon as possible in order to avoid being trapped.

The dragon goes through the next several walls without slowing down, eventually reaching the vendor hall. Jesse yanks on the reins, turning the chariot towards the lobby area as the dragon card returns to the deck. The way is now blocked with the metal riot doors. Artemis pulls out the Dragon World card and tosses it in front.

The card roars to life as it slams through the metal doors as well as the entire glass façade of the hotel before roaring off into the sky. Christine shields herself from the raining glass as the chariot passes through the opening. Survivors scream or curse as they panic, diving or jumping to clear the way for speeding beasts. Jesse pulls back on the reins, commanding the sphinxes to stop. The beasts yowl as they lock their legs and sit down in order to halt both themselves and the chariot they pull. The vehicle comes to rest in front of Lawson.

"Hello fellas, looks like you've had a hard run," Lawson addresses the sphinxes.

The chariot disappears, dropping the passengers to the ground. Jesse collapses to her knees, panting heavily as her skin continues to show signs of burning. She looks up as Lawson bends down to check on her. She sees him frown at her condition. Artemis touches Jesse with a frown and pulls back from both the heat and smoke emitting from the woman.

"You're burning," Artemis said and looks around. "Diana!"

"Mr. Trunic," Jesse addresses the man, "you have to get the sprinklers going, the Flames of Madness and their mistress are still strong in that hotel."

"Flames of Madness?" Lawson asks. He becomes concerned when Jesse does not answer.

Diana arrives next to the group as Jesse passes out, crumbling to the ground. She touches the unconscious woman and draws her hand back, shaking it. Diana briefly thinks about the ambulance behind her then grabs hold of Jesse and disappears in a rain of golden dust. Lawson stands up and looks at the building, inadvertently ignoring Christine for now. She notices this and tries to slip away. Her escape never happens when her feet do not disobey her commands. She glances over at Artemis and notices that the deity is concentrating on the building as well, where it appears that a storm is brewing. Christine feels the bottom of her stomach tank as she turns the other way and meets the gaze of Deloris as Lawson walks away.

"I think you need to sit tight, Officer Christine Longstraw," Deloris says as she folds her arms.

"Officer Moody," Lawson says to his subordinate. "I need for you to hack into the sprinkler system."

"On it," Moody acknowledges as he sits on the ground and begins to manipulate the keys on the computer provided to him by Louis.

"Dang, that's an old beast," Lawson notes the computer.

"Dr. Lygtbut said it got past Charlie to get them out," Moody says. "I hope it has another trick for the sprinklers. My review of Charlie's history indicates that he rarely gets defeated twice by the same tactics."

"Get them going, I don't care how you do it," Lawson reiterates as he walks to his next destination. "Mr. Kalup Leyman, can you elaborate on the Flames of Madness and what the hell just happened in your hotel?"

"I just survived a massacre, and you have the gall to ask me these questions now?" Kalup snaps. "I have no idea what the Flames of Madness are and anything else will have to wait until I talk to my lawyer."

"I honestly think that any lawyer with half the intellect of a sponge will not touch this case with a ten-foot pole," Lawson said. "I will give you a little time to relax, then I will be back for a few answers."

Lightning strikes the building several times, yet nothing catches on fire. Deloris watches the unusual storm for a moment then turns when she hears Lawson approaching. Artemis glances at the commissioner and moves a step or two to the right to prevent him from running into her. She remains invisible to him. Lawson watches the storm for a minute then turns his attention to Christine. She bites back a swear word as he approaches her but does not hide the relief she feels when Deloris does not follow him. She even feels the vampress' grip loosen upon her.

"Christine, you and I have to talk," Lawson says.

"About what?" Christine challenges. "I didn't do anything wrong."

"That, in itself, is the wrong answer and attitude to have in this situation," Lawson warns. "We are going to discuss your vacation habits and disposition during this crisis. I want you to explain to me why a civilian had to step up and do the duties of a PIU officer when one was in the building."

"I was going to do it, but she volunteered," Christine said, a slight whine in her words.

"That's not what I have," Lawson said and holds up his phone. He replays the recording with both Christine and Jesse when they were in the church.

"You... recorded that conversation?" Christine asks, flabbergasted.

"I record everything," Lawson responds. "I'm waiting."

"I..." Christine starts then sneers. "You can't do anything to me, I'm a special assignment by Councilman Harry. I..."

"Another wrong answer," Lawson interrupts, irritation in his voice. "Since you are unwilling to talk to me about it..." He looks over toward Deloris.

"No wait, I'll talk to you," Christine blurts out before he could call over the vampire.

"Intelligent choice," Lawson remarks.

Meanwhile, L. A. Moody types in a few more commands and hits the enter button. The computer pauses a moment as it reads the instructions. All of the processors on board start up with every available fan within the laptop ramped up to full speed. The screen flickers several times then pauses on the cellular network. It goes to battle trying to force itself in then gives up and goes to several other networks.

Several moments would pass before it pauses and pops up a box requesting permission to go onto nearby networks. L.A. checks the networks the computer brings up, selects all but Tanglewood Hospital, and once again hits enter. The machine ramps up once again as it goes through the other networks and backdoors into the hotel's main intranet. The processers go into overdrive as the computer battles on three fronts. Several minutes later, the computer's fans begin to slow down as its processing speed wanes. A siren and ringing bells emit from the hotel as the sound of water whooshing in large quantities fills the air, starting on the ground floor. The computer presents a pop up on the screen with one simple word: Success.

CHAPTER TEN

Guardians and Demons

The elements of lightning and fire rip through the upper floors of the hotel as the battle reaches a fever pitch. Aegis blocks the flames sent to him then destroys them in one swipe of his blade. Irava sneers at him as she cracks her whip, aiming for his neck. The weapon cracks and cackles as it sails through the air. It makes a disappointed sound when it hits nothing as the intended target disappears.

Irava turns into flames and moves as fast as the fire when Aegis reappears and swings his sword, intending to take off her head. The fire shifts as she changes forms into the Beast of Flames and roars, exhaling a stream of blood-red fire at the Guardian. Aegis holds the hilt in one hand and presses the flat of the blade against the other then braces. The flames slam into the blade and move around the Guardian, transforming into steam.

The steam increases until it cloaks the entire floor in a sickly green fog. The mist occasionally forms into laughing faces. Aegis looks around, his senses on high alert as he searches for his quarry. A whip cracks and wraps around his blade, yanking it away from him. Aegis curses then turns and holds his arm up as the beast attacks. She chomps down on the armored forearm of the Guardian and increases pressure in an effort to break or rip it off.

Alarms shrill out seconds before the sprinklers come on full blast. The beast shrieks in pain and anger as the water pours down, saturating the entire floor. Aegis grabs the beast with his free hand and uses his wings to propel them forward to a distant wall at unheard-of speed. They go through the first wall, an interior one, and destroy the computers used by Charlie. The entire hotel goes black as Aegis crashes through a second interior wall then rams through the exterior wall.

Witnesses on the ground gasp as they look up at the plume of dust and debris exiting the 100th floor of the hotel. Lawson glances at the sight and shouts to the people closest to the plume to retreat. The huge group of witnesses hastily obey the orders as large blocks of thick glass and mortar hit and bury deeply into the ground. Wayward chucks of debris are deflected, landing very close to survivors thanks to the efforts of the PIU team. One of the male members of the force yells for the group to move back further. His orders are hastily obeyed.

Lawson retreats to check on the group as Artemis focuses on the clearing cloud. She arches an eyebrow and swears as she jumps back, giving way to the creature that Aegis had just tossed to the ground. The Beast of the Flames land and slides back a few inches before regaining her feet. Aegis glares down at his opponent, a look of pure rage upon his features.

The Beast, Irava, sneers back at the Guardian then lights up, flames crisp anything within five feet of her. Irava tilts her head back and shrieks, deafening those that were not touched by the flames. The survivors that had been burned by the Flames of Madness begin to laugh maniacally as they once again light afire. They run to Irava, jump into the flames surrounding her and are consumed in an instant. Bat-like wings sprout from the beast's back as she launches into the air, aiming for the Guardian. A golden arrow slam into Irava's flank. She grunts but is otherwise unaffected.

Artemis scowls at the results as she pulls back on her bow again. The Tarot card, Eight of Staffs, appear in her drawing hand as well as another arrow, then she releases them. The arrow elongates into the size of a spear and multiplies into eight while flying to the target. All eight hit the Beast of Flames, penetrating the tough hide easily. Irava screams in pain as she crashes back down to the ground. The shafts of the spear-like arrows turn into ashes as fire consumes them. The beast turns her attention toward Kalup and charges forward. The hotel tycoon curses as he takes several steps back.

A rope made from lightning wraps around the Beast of Flames and drags her back towards the hotel. Irava shrieks in surprise and anger as she is raked across the ground. She digs her talons in to stop her slide and struggle to her feet. Irava screams as she morphs into flames. The rope goes slack, slipping through the element. The beast returns, standing on her hind legs and takes aim at the Guardian. She roars as she exhales her fire breath. It is cut short when another set of spears slam her on the side. The beast screeches and turns towards the perpetrator.

Artemis lifts her bow with one more card in hand, the Eight of Swords, then releases it, aiming just above the beast. Irava jumps forward to attack her captor. She rams into a gigantic blade that blocks her path. A roar of rage escapes her as she scrambles backwards. Her hindquarter is sliced as she touches another blade. She notices she is surrounded by blades whose handles resemble the shafts of arrows. The beast turns into flames to try and rush past the cage. She makes a surprised sound when she is forced to return to the beast shape, still inside of the impromptu cage. The swords begin to glow as Artemis concentrates upon them.

In the sky above, Aegis watches the Beast of Flames struggle to get free herself from the cage. He calls his sword to his hand. His wings spread out wide as he flaps them once, then folds them tight against his body. The Guardian drops straight down with the tip of his sword aimed at Irava's skull. A cone of light appears around him as he continues his descent. The beast bellows as she concentrates on Artemis. Irava meet the deity's gaze and start to hack out an incantation. She does not notice Aegis until his sword goes through her head, cutting her words short. The Guardian stands on the neck of the Beast of Flames, pulls his sword out of the skull, and decapitates it.

A high-pitched sound erupts from the beast's body as it melts into the ground. Aegis jumps back as the earth where the beast died erupts. A stream of red-light shoot into the hotel as the bricks take on the same angry glow. The building rumbles as the illumination pulsate between red and white. The white light coagulates and shoots from the top of the hotel straight into the sky. Clouds gather around the stream as it splits into three.

A red-light arch over and slams into the ground where the Beast of Flames died. The original white light continues to fly upwards as another, brighter, light encircles it. The third light turns black and slams back into the hotel. Minutes later, the three lights fade then disappear. Aegis sheaths his sword as his golden armor turns into light and floats towards the heavens. The blades surrounding him also disappear, returning to card form. Artemis picks up the Tarot card and places it back in the deck where it belongs. The quaking of the building ceases as everything quiets back down.

"Alright, I have to know," Lawson says. He turns to his senior officer. "Deloris, what the heck was that?"

"For once, I do not have an answer," Deloris responds honestly.

"The beast was the Mistress of the Flames," Aegis said as he approaches the commissioner. "Her name was Irava. She is dead. The lights were the releasing of souls. The white is salvation, the red is damnation, and the black is the undecided."

"This Irava was responsible for the fiasco in the hotel?" Lawson asks.

"In part, but you may want to speak to Kalup for his role. In desperation, the beast did try to merge with him," Aegis says.

"You are a Guardian," Deloris observes. "Where is your twin?"

"I'm sure he's around," Aegis answers with a smile. "Excuse me." He walks away.

Aegis approaches Artemis, hesitating a few feet from her. She turns and crosses her arms as the Guardian bows his head in respect and thanks. Artemis nods in response and watches as Aegis uses his wings to take to the skies once more. The Guardian disappears into the clouds. Lawson watches the sight then turns when he hears the ambulance leave the scene. Apparently, Kalup has fainted, and they are taking the hotel tycoon to the hospital. Deloris catches his attention when she calls to the other officers to assist the new batch of survivors that are exiting the hotel.

Two weeks later, beeps and soft voices reach the ears of the unconscious woman. Jesse coaxes herself awake, opening her eyes. Her sight is foggy at first. She blinks until she is able to focus upon the sterile white walls of a luxury hospital room. The rays of the sun shine through the large window, highlighting stainless steel rods that circle the ceiling. Jesse grits her teeth as she slides her elbows under her and pushes up in an effort to raise her head.

A soft whirl catches her ear moments before the top half of the bed raises to meet her back. She places her arms beside her and relaxes as the mechanisms continue to move until she is sitting up. Jesse rubs her right hand over her left arm and pauses when she feels a slightly painful tug. She looks down to see two IVs, one in each arm, and visually traces the plastic tubing back to three different bags of liquids.

Jesse pulls back the sheet from her legs to study them. She notices that she has a strange design upon her shin, almost like branches in a small, upside-down tree. Jesse moves her ankles and feels the click in the damaged one but no pain. She lifts a hand to her head as she tries to figure out what has happened to her. She once again pauses when she feels more pressure on her IVs. She relaxes and tilts her head forward to meet her hand instead. Her eyes widen when she feels a large, soft, bandage in place of her hair.

"Where....am I?" Jesse says in a whisper. A polite beep sounds as a green 'nurse' light illuminate.

There is a gentle knock on the door before it opens to allow two visitors to walk into the room. Jesse studies them and recognizes the smallest one as a grey and white seraph cat. A white streak on her nose highlights her light green human-like eyes. The cat's assistant is a young human girl with the word 'intern' stitched onto her nurse's coat. The head nurse hops up onto a table located on the side of Jesse's bed and studies the patient.

"Hello, Ms. Monroe, I am glad you are finally awake," the seraph cat says. "I am Kelly, your nurse. How are you feeling?"

"I am fine, Ms. Kelly," Jesse answers. "I'm a bit perplexed at all the medical equipment around me."

"When you arrived, you were burning," Kelly informs her as she sits down, her fluffy tail waving, patiently. "Dr. Lygtbut took you to surgery right away, he just basically finished a few hours ago."

"Hours ago," Jesse frowns. "How long was the surgery?"

"It was very long, but he did it in multiple stages and not straight through," Kelly said. "We have Dr. Geno to thank for that. No human I know can survive a two-week marathon surgery if it is straight through."

"Two week what?" Jesse shouts, taken aback by the news.

"Good, that got your blood pressure up, I'm glad you are doing better," Kelly smiles. "I will let Dr. Lygtbut know you are ready to see him."

Kelly instructs her intern on the other vitals to take and type them up in the patient's chart. The two attentive nurses finish their duties then pack up their equipment. Kelly taps a button on the bed to cancel the nurse call button. She then hops down off the table and saunters from the room, followed by her assistant.

Jesse watches them leave then closes her eyes to relax. She opens them just in time to see a third nurse slip through the doorway. Jesse stares at the woman then hisses as the back of her neck tingles, indicating danger. The patient focuses on the nurse and swears as the woman stalks closer.

The intruder has charred skin as well as the outfit from the sanitarium. Jesse recognizes the nurse specter from the hotel and once again curses as she reaches for the call button. The remote flies away from her hands.

"How is it that you are able to travel from the site of your unfortunate demise, woman?" Jesse demands, then hesitates as she deduces the answer to her own question. "You are one of the Mistress's minions."

"Or am I her creator," the nurse ghost says with a hiss.

The ghoul stands next to Jesse's bed with a menacing grin as she reaches into her pocket. She pulls out a large needle filled with a strange, clear liquid. Her face stretches and her eyes widen from madness as she reaches for the IV tube. A large hand grabs the nurse ghost, surprising both Jesse and her nemesis.

The ghoul's features go from insanity to pure shock as she gazes at the person that interrupted her devious attempt. Jesse follows the specter's line of sight and smiles. Aegis scowls at the ghost as he lifts her up, his wings spread wide in annoyance. The

Guardian snorts as he effortlessly tosses the nurse towards the door. She is caught by an invisible force which holds her fast.

Jesse turns when she hears the nurse ghost holler as she struggles, unable to escape. The invisible man comes into view as Jesse stares at him. He appears to be a twin of Aegis; except he has black horns protruding from his forehead and large wings of the same color spreading from his back. He meets the Guardian's gaze and nods a greeting. Aegis returns the gesture before his twin and the nurse ghost sink into the floor. The ghost's struggles and sounds are cut short as she is pulled to her final destination. Aegis picks up the discarded needle and destroys it.

"You don't know how glad I am to see you, Aegis," Jesse says to the Guardian.

"I can read it in your smile," Aegis responds. "That you are awake and smiling is joyful to me. The Mistress of the Flame, Irava, is dead."

"Thank goodness," Jesse lets her head fall back briefly, then sits back up. "What about Nako?"

"Sir Nako is doing well," Louis says and leans against the doorframe when he gathers the attention of the room. "The old cat is trying to flirt with a few members of my staff. I had to have a discussion with him before I came down here."

"Louis," Jesse greets him with a smile. "You're not a dragon anymore."

"Always a dragon," Louis assures her with a chuckle. "Just not in that form right now. Aegis, I see you are still standing sentinel."

"Always a Guardian," Aegis agrees.

"Of course," Louis says, sitting on the foot of the bed. "Jesse, have you tried to walk yet?"

"Not yet, I just woke up a not that long ago," Jesse said.

"Well, before I make you stand, let me check you over. Your surgery took quite a while," Louis stands as he explains. "I had to replace a large portion of nerves on the left side of your body."

Jesse stares at Louis as he continues to explain the process he used to stop her from burning. The doctor even surprises his patient by reporting that her ankle injury contributed to the condition. Louis looks over the bandages, pleased to see that the bleeding has slowed down. Jesse inquiries about her head. The doctor examines her noggin and sits down to look her in the eye.

"I had to shave your head to get to the source of the burning," Louis said. "I also had to start there and work my way down as I replaced the damaged nerves with new hybrid nerve."

"So, I am a cyborg?" Jesse asks.

"No, you are still human. The hybridization stems from combining Aligon and human cells and they are grown in a lab," Louis assures her. "Because of your advanced mystical abilities, I believe that the hybrid is much better for you. You will recover your abilities faster."

"What are the side effects?" Jesse asks.

"From what I have seen in other patients, they are not bad," Louis assures her. "When your hair grows back, you will have multiple tones. The left eye will be a shade darker or lighter than usual. We will evaluate more when you start practicing your magic again."

"How much longer must I stay in the hospital?" Jesse presses.

"At least another three days. I want to make sure you are able to walk and navigate short distances before I release you into the care of Aegis," Louis says. "He has volunteered to help nurse you back to health."

"My skills extend beyond demon killing," Aegis speaks up with a smile as Jesse stares at him.

"Okay," Jesse rubs the bridge of her nose with one hand. "I'm ready, get me up."

Jesse places her hands beside her and tries to push herself to the edge of the bed to no avail. Aegis picks her up and, with great care, places her on her feet. She wobbles, her body seems unready for the sudden change in height. Louis steadies her as she takes her first, unsteady, step. Aegis stands on the opposite side and helps guide Jesse to the small couch facing a blank wall. The holotube automatically pops on as she sits down on the couch. Jesse trembles a little bit but is unsure if she is cold or in pain. Aegis sits down next to the woman and places a blanket across her shoulders. Louis checks her vitals as the news interrupts a nature show.

"Breaking news on this Friday, November 13th," the male news anchor says. "Hotel tycoon Kalup Leyman has entered a not guilty plea in the cases and lawsuits against him. We turn to Liz for details."

"Thank you, Gary," an older woman in an expensive dress suit replaces the man. "To recap, Kalup Leyman has been accused of allowing the summoning of demons to destroy countless lives within his flagship hotel, the Grand Leyman. He is also allegedly responsible for the destruction of Our Holy Father Megachurch for The Faithful as well as the Museum of Past Modern History's

School of Metaphysical Arts. The latter formally known as the Monroe College of Metamorphism."

Jesse's jaw drops upon hearing the news. The holotube then shows the various locations as the newswoman continues to talk. The Grand Leyman Hotel and Casino is shown first, the ruins still smoldering on the upper floors, half of it has fallen. The camera crew goes inside to show broken furniture and scattered trinkets mixing in with body parts from various creatures.

Security bots shut the camera down and, in haste, escort the crew out. The next location is the megachurch; the scene shows the massive building has been reduced to rubble, and the camera cuts over to the college as a surviving Faithful spews angry word about witches. Jesse's heart sinks to the floor when she sees the massive college destroyed, to include her family home.

"It...was not a bad dream," Jesse whispers as tears swell in her eyes.

"I'm so sorry, Jesse, that you had to see that," Louis turns off the holotube.

"This means that she is now without a home," Aegis frowns.

Jesse finally breaks down, unable to contain her anguish within. Aegis gently pulls the emotional woman into his arms and holds her close. His left wing encircles her within a soft yet strong comfortable embrace as well. Louis places a hand upon Jesse's shoulder in solidarity. The doctor stands up shortly afterwards and goes to the door when he hears someone scratching at it. He opens it and looks down at a patiently waiting Nako. The curator stretches before he walks in and heads over to Jesse.

"Assume you saw the news, Sir Nako," Louis addresses the cat.

"I did, and will not repeat my initial words," Nako said. "My first thought, however, is to check on Jesse."

"Jesse, you have a small furry visitor," Aegis says softly to the woman.

Nako jumps up onto the arm of the couch as Jesse composes herself and takes a deep breath in. Aegis folds his wing back as the woman sits up and turns to face her visitor. Jesse smiles and hugs the seraph cat, much to Nako's delight. He wiggles to get free from her grip and does his happy jig when she sits back. Nako prances on all four paws as he turns in place, his tail and wings moving excitedly. Jesse could not help but chuckle at the antics of the flamboyant feline.

"Much better," Nako says of Jesse's smile. "I saw the news. I wanted to come and personally offer you my residence until we are able to rebuild your school and home."

"What? Are you sure, Nako?" Jesse asks.

"Prior to the fiasco of the hotel, you were brought on as Curator to the Museum of Past Modern History's School of Metaphysical Arts." Nako reminds her. "Per the documents that you signed, I am responsible for the buildings, and everything associated with them. I am also responsible for making sure you have a comfortable place to live by virtue of my own cognancies. My home is also registered under the museum system, it's an architectural antique."

"Nako, are you sure she will be comfortable there? Your house is haunted," Louis reminds him.

"Not as haunted since Deloris helped get rid of some of the more unsavory spirits," Nako replies.

"Whatever the officer did not get rid of, I can finish," Aegis volunteers. "Jesse needs a place to recover."

"What choices do I have?" Jesse said with a helpless shrug.

"I can always call Queen Arayna, I'm sure she would not mind hosting you at the Aligon palace," Louis volunteers. He looks down at his wristwatch and frowns. "Speaking of Her Majesty, it looks like she just saw the news article as well. I am being summoned to the virtual conference room."

"I'll go with you in a minute Louis, I'm sure she wants to speak to us both," Nako says. "Jesse, can I expect your company?"

"Yes, Sir Nako, I accept your hospitality," Jesse relents.

She smiles when Nako does another dance and spins around. He slips and instantly digs his claws in to prevent from falling off the arm of the couch. The seraph cat then jumps down and pats his paws on the floor before leading the way to the door. He chirps excitedly as he trots gallantly from the room. Louis rolls his eyes with a smile then follows the happy feline. The door closes as Jesse goes over what had happened in the moments since she awakened.

A couple of hours later, there is a knock on the door awakening Jesse from a nap. She blinks and looks around in a moment of confusion. She then realizes that she is using Aegis as a pillow. The Guardian is humored when Jesse apologizes and tries to sit up. He helps her by moving, relinquishing corner of the couch so that he could slide her over. Aegis then stands behind Jesse as she beckons the visitor to enter.

The door opens as two people walk through. Jesse recognizes the PIU officer, Diana Hunter, but not the tall man that follows her in. He closes the door behind and smiles warmly at the patient. Jesse studies the man, noting that he seems to be either a warlock or a vampire. Maybe both from the strong power vibe she detects from him. He has black hair and matching well-kept beard. Light gray eyes hold wisdom as well as humor within them. He is wearing an expensive black suit with a red tie. His shoes are glossy from the shine, a result of a fresh wax job He is carrying a large duffle bag. Jesse scans the room, searching for one more visitor.

"Good afternoon, Curator Monroe," Diana greets her with a smile. "I am glad you are awake and appear to be in good health."

"I'm awake but I am working on getting better," Jesse says. "Thank you for visiting. Who is with you?"

"Artemis is here but it looks like you cannot see her," Diana observes.

"Sadly, no," Jesse admits. "Louis told me that a lot of my abilities will have to be relearned."

"A great deal of them, from my understanding," Aegis said. "I've been instructed to help you recover them, slowly."

"That would be best," the second man in the room said.

"I'm sorry, I did not get your name," Jesse focuses on him.

"Apologies, I was just listening," the man says as he puts his bag down and walks over to offer a hand. "I am Sir Hershel Matox, an elite Knight of the Galactic University of Mystical Artists."

"You are Deloris's ex-husband," Diana deduces.

"You are a vampire," Jesse says at the same time.

"Yes, on both accounts." Hershel chuckles. "I am also the lawyer that my order has assigned to your case to fully represent and protect you to the fullest extent of the law. I've been informed to provide any other assistance that you may need."

"So, you will be staying while I talk to Ms. Monroe about her experiences," Diana concludes.

"Yes, I am." Hershel smile, briefly flashing his vampric teeth. "Providing that she is up to the conversation."

"What's going on?" Jesse asks, cautiously. She watches as Diana closes her eyes and exhales to regain her calm.

"Right," Diana said. "We are here for a couple of reasons. One is a social visit, both Artemis and I were concerned when you exited the hotel. I'm also here to start an investigation into Officer Christine Longstraw's behavior during the crisis within the Grand Leyman Hotel and Casino."

"She behaved like a spoiled brat," Jesse said. "But I am willing to elaborate as long as I have strength to do so."

"Great. Before we start, I am told to return your Tarot decks to you," Diana said and pulls the two decks out of her pocket, placing them on the table. "Per Sir Nako's request, we were also able to retrieve this."

Jesse's curiosity soon gives way to surprise as Diana places a framed photograph in her hands. Jesse tears up again when she gazes at the picture of her ten-year-old self, grandmother, and mother all smiling at the camera. A Siamese kitten is sitting in her grandmother's lap and appears to also grin for the camera. Jesse closes her eyes and hugs the photograph to her chest. She opens her eyes and focuses on Diana, mouthing words of thanks.

"You are more than welcome, Ms. Monroe," Diana says as a chair slides up behind her and she sits down.

"That reminds me, I have a very special guest," Hershel says as he bends down and unzips his duffel bag. The head of an old

Siamese cat pops out as she looks around with wide eyes. She has the same markings as the one in the picture.

"Aunt Aggie!" Jesse says as cheerful tears flow.

The cat meows as she daintily steps out of the bag and stretches. The old cat takes her time walking to the couch and sits. She meows a few times before Aegis smiles and uses a wing to help her up onto the seat. Jesse places a hand over her mouth as she gently rubs the old Earth cat. Aggie purrs and settles down next to Jesse to continue her nap. Hershel picks the bag up and causes it to disappear as he studies the situation.

"Donner rescued Lady Aggie before the demolition bot could destroy your home. He suffered greatly at her claws, apparently the Lady does not like to be disturbed," Hershel offers. "I see that you are very emotional, Ms. Monroe, should Officer Hunter and I return at a later time?"

"No, I'm Okay," Jesse wipes the tears away. "Let's talk, Diana. I've got a lot to say about Christine, Kalup and the entire fiasco."

"Yes ma'am," Diana said as she crosses her legs and brings up an application on her phone orb to take notes. Artemis sits on the couch next to Jesse and uses a soft touch to scratch Aunt Aggie behind the ears. The cat purrs.

"I will start with the meeting with Irava and Ronan," Jesse said.

"You may not need to worry about Ronan," Aegis said. "His fate is tied with the Mistress of the Flames."

The media speaks mercilessly about the tragedies of the Grand Leyman Hotel and the megachurch with wild theories involving the metaphysical school. Between the disasters is coverage for the trial against Kalup Leyman. His plea of innocence and the resulting ruckus is cut short when Ronan turns off his holotube with a snort. He had just finished talking to an investigator about his experiences. Ronan insisted that he is innocent and just a pawn used by Irava to program the Ouija software. He had jumped for joy when the investigator told him that Irava is dead. The federal agent then left without arresting the programmer.

As soon as the investigator had left, Ronan retreated to his lair, the basement of his mother's home. The phone rings and he hear his mother answer it, curse at the caller and hang up. Ronan shakes his head as he reaches inside a stool and pulls out his secondary laptop. He frowns at it; the thing will need to be updated before he can reopen his programing business. The phone rings again as Ronan searches for the power cord to the computer.

"RONAN!" a shrill, frail, female voice hollers at him from upstairs. "You have a phone call from the PIU, did you want to take it?"

"No ma, I'm busy!" Ronan calls back.

"She sounds sexy, you might want to talk to her," his mother insists. "You need to get out and find some new friends anyway."

"No, Ma. I don't want to talk to her. I'm trying to get my backup computer to run," Ronan reiterates. "Besides, how do you know what sexy is?"

"I met your father and you're here, right?" his mother retaliates.

"I'm busy, ma," Ronan repeats and decides to ignore his mother.

Ronan sets his computer down and plugs it into the outlet before opening it. It beeps at him as the screen lights up and goes through the diagnosis. Ronan exhales impatiently as he stands up to go to a makeshift kitchen and fix himself some instant noodles. He swears when he notices the only ones left are tuna flavored, his least favorite. Grumbling, he treks to the storage room as the computer continues to boot up.

A holographic keyboard illuminates on the table and switches from QWERTY to a strange runic language. Ghostly hands type in a password then a few other commands. Charlie appears in the screen at first then leaps out into the room. The ghost grins then disappear as the young programmer comes back into the room and opens a can of instant rice. Ronan pops it in the microwave then walks back to his computer. He takes one look at his screen and rolls his eyes at the audacity of an amateur stupidly hacking into his computer.

"Whoever you are, you are going down," Ronan says confidently as he sits down in front of the computer.

The screen goes from green to blue as Ronan types in several commands. He hesitates when he notices the keyboard he is typing on. Swearing, he stands up as the screen turns red and tormented voices scream from within. Ronan takes a nearly twenty steps back and turns try to escape the image. He screams instead when he comes face to face with Charlie.

Shaking with fear the young man calls out to his mother as the ghost snickers. No one upstairs answers his calls. Charlie licks his lips before ensnaring his victim with the belts of the straitjacket. Ronan tries to scream again but no sound escapes his throat. Charlie laughs maniacally as he reaches inside of Ronan's mouth with several belts and yanks out his soul.

The programmer's body falls to the floor as the spirit screams to be free. Charlie makes a sound of glee as he dives back into the computer, dragging Ronan's life force with him. The programmer's body flops over with a strange tattoo written into his forehead. Blood squirts from it, covering the floor. Charlie's laughter echoes in the basement along with the screams of various victims.

"Ronan! Stop all that noise! A body can't think when you play those stupid video games," Ronan's mother shouts from above.

Charlie peeks out and looks around like a naughty child. He grins as he disappears once more. The keys on the computer move a few times. The computer emits a beep of acknowledgment as it shuts down and goes dead. The microwave beeps as it finishes cooking the meal. Lights dim then shut down altogether when no movement is detected. The blood from Ronan's body spreads out and spells an ominous message upon the carpet: Betrayal means death.